CONTENTS

DAMAGED GOODS

Part One

Angela Peña

Dedication
*For my mother Roseann and every person who was strong
enough to say enough,
I dedicate this book to you. I will never forget your strength and
bravery that day. As a child you taught me so many things like
having compassion for others. You also taught me not to take
anyone's shit. Though you are no longer here, I carry you with me
in my heart and my spirit forever.
I love you.*

PROLOGUE

I am so tired I can't open my eyes. I hear a faint beeping some-where and all I want is for it to stop. That's when I hear a voice I recognize. It's my best friend, Kate. She's crying. I struggle to open my eyes, but I can't. I fight with everything I have, but my body isn't cooperating. She's talking again. I try hard to focus on her words. She's telling me not to leave her, something I find weird because I can't even open my eyes because of how tired I am. How could I leave her? Again, I fight a losing battle trying to open my eyes. I feel her hand on mine, but I'm so disoriented I can't move my fingers.

"Maddie, I love you. I need you to fight Babe. Stay with me. You're all I have." She's crying.

I try to tell her I'm here. I want to comfort her, but I can't get the words out. I'm frustrated. I promised Kate I would never leave her and the pain in her voice is breaking my heart. It makes me so sad that I can feel tears in my eyes. They fall down my cheek. I feel her hand go to my face, wiping the tears away. She says my name over and over. I'm trying so hard to let her know I am here and I can hear her. I want to tell her I'll never leave her but I can't and that makes me angry. Hearing her this sad and not being able to com-fort her is torture. Just knowing something I am doing is hurting her makes me fight the sleepiness. I fight it. I shake myself as I struggle to open my eyes. Why can't I open my eyes? I panic. Kate's hands slip away from my face as I hear her yell. "Nurse." She cries. Then I feel her squeezing and rubbing my hand. "Come on, Mad-die. Fight, damn it. Come back to me."

I'm fighting Kate. I'm trying. I think as I struggle against the sleepiness. My eyes open and I look around. I'm in Gram's kitchen. It smells like her chocolate chip cookies. I inhale deep because I've missed that delicious scent so much. I haven't been able to make them since she passed. I miss her too much and it still hurts so bad not having her.

"Madison." The sound of Gram's voice startles me because she's been dead for six months. She's now sitting across from me looking worried.

"Gram." I wonder if I am losing it.

"Yes, baby. It's me."

"How is this possible?" I ask as she reaches over, taking my hand. The same hand Kate was just holding.

"Something happened, baby. Something bad."

"Am I dead?" I panic as I squeeze her hand.

"No, baby, but you need to fight. I know you're tired but you need to open those beautiful brown eyes for me."

"I can't Gram something's wrong. I'm so tired."

"Baby, you have to."

"Dean, he..." I can't get the words out.

"I know, baby."

"This isn't right, you need to wake up. You need to fight. It's not your time. Kate needs you."

"I know. I tried to tell her I'm here. She can't hear me."

"You need to wake up, Madison. Fight!"

"I'm trying its hard. I can't open my eyes."

"Fight Madison. You can't come here, not yet. Something better is waiting for you. I've seen it. Wake up."

The beeping from earlier is back. Gram stands. She walks to the door. "Gram, where are you going?"

"Where I belong, honey. Now wake up Kate needs you. I'll be watching." She smiles at me.

"Gram don't leave!" I yell as she walks to the door.

I lunge for the door she's going through, but it shuts quickly behind her. Just like that, she disappears. I jolt awake at the sound of it slamming. Kate's tear-streaked face comes into view. Her nose is red from crying, but she's smiling. I look over and see the source of the beeping. It's a monitor at the side of my bed. I'm in the hospital. Immediately my hand goes to my belly. It doesn't feel right. Something's wrong. Gram was right, something terrible happened. One look in Kate's eyes and I just know.

CHAPTER ONE

Madison

I am making dinner as I watch the baseball game when Kate comes out of her bedroom and does a twirl.

"How do I look?" She strikes a seductive pose.

"Like a very fancy lawyer going to a very expensive dinner with her boyfriend."

"Oh my God, that's exactly what I was going for!" Her tone is sarcastic as her hands go to her hips. I can't help but laugh. We are literally the odd couple, me in my t-shirt and leggings, my hair in a super messy bun, not a stitch of make-up on. Kate in a lovely blue evening gown that makes her big blue eyes pop more than they usually do.

"Just kidding you look smoking hot!" I smile wide and wink at her. "Can I be safe to assume you will not be coming home tonight?" I wiggle my brows at her before I turn to the stove to stir my soup again.

"I better not be! We haven't spent the night together in over a week with our schedules being so crazy. I plan on this dress spending the night on his bedroom floor."

"You should at least drape it over a chair or something."

Kate scrunches her face as I shrug, turning back to the stove.

"What it looks expensive." I tease as I stir my soup.

"Honestly, he could rip it off of my body at this rate. I am so horny I might jump him in the limo."

We both laugh. That's when we hear it. Someone clears their

throat from behind Kate. I turn to see what I imagine her best impression of a bug might be. Her eyes are wide and she looks like she wants to run and hide. I look past her to Eric, his colleague, and what I can only assume is his colleagues' date. The man beside him does his best to hide his smile. The woman seems unamused. Eric has a key, so he let himself and his friends in. The roar of the game must have drowned out their arrival.

"Hey, Eric." I do my best to hold my laugh as I continue stirring my soup. I grab the remote and lower the volume of the game.

"Hey, Maddie." He walks over to Kate and wraps his arms around her, kissing her cheek. He whispers something in her ear causing her to smile. I have a feeling he's assuring her they are on for later tonight. Kate excuses herself to grab her clutch.

"Maddie." Eric looks over at me. "This is Hawthorne Price and his lovely girlfriend, Irina Vonn."

"Nice to meet you both." I walk over, wiping my hands on a dishtowel and then holding one out to greet them. Hawthorne takes my hand immediately. God, he is gorgeous. I look up into the biggest brown eyes I've ever seen and then he smiles. He is the definition of tall, dark and handsome. He's the total opposite of Dean's all-American boy next door look. Irina doesn't seem enthused with our prolonged contact. She quickly redirects things with a tight smile. "We should go, or we'll be late." She steps in, placing her hand on Hawthorne's chest. That's when I realize he's still holding my hand. I shake myself before pulling back. Hawthorne doesn't avert his gaze from me. I feel my cheeks flush. I'm embarrassed by how long I lingered. I offer Irina my hand, and she literally leaves me hanging. I lower it and blink a few times, trying to process what just happened between myself and Hawthorne and then with Irina. Thankfully, Kate hadn't seen it, but Eric did, and that makes what he says next awkward.

"Hawthorne, Maddie would be a great fit to replace your personal assistant. She has a degree in communications, you know."

"You do." Irina said as if it surprised her I could read and write.

Her eyes travel up and down my body. As if the way I look or dress would somehow change my ability to use my brain. I bet this woman has never worn a pair of leggings in her life and probably didn't own a single t-shirt. Looking at her in that gown I bet she didn't eat carbs either.

"Yes, I do." I reply, trying not to let her get to me. Bitch! Too late. Great, my inner monologue is coming out to play. I need a job though, so the mini me in my head has to be cool. It's not like I'd see her there if I got it, right? No, she's probably too busy shopping and doing photoshoots. My mini me is probably right.

"We should set up an interview my last assistant left abruptly." He peeks over at Irina for a moment. I bet this one's sparkling personality had something to do with that. My mini me is taking a seat and making herself comfy. My heart sinks because I'm sure if I get this I won't last long. If Irina has anything to say about it, it probably won't happen. No doubt these inside thoughts would eventually break their way out if I have to deal with her.

"Sure, that'd be great." I give him a polite smile.

"I'll get your info from Kate, and I'll call you to schedule." I nod, thinking there is no way in hell he will call me. It makes me a little sad because I need a job so I can get out of Kate's place. By the look on Irina's face, I'm sure he'll be hearing the reasons he won't be hiring me later tonight. Kate smiles as she returns from grabbing her clutch. "I'm all set". She smiles up at Eric. Eric seems pleased with himself as he hooks an arm around Kate's waist. I wonder if my presence is the reason he's spent so little time with her over the last month. The guilt of the burden our friendship is putting on Kate's life lights a fire under my ass. I need to speed getting a job up. Health-wise I am almost one hundred percent, mentally I'm a mess. She lowers her brows at me as she comes over, kissing my cheek. She knows me too well.

"I'll see you later." She hesitates, studying my face.

"You better not." I whisper in her ear as I hug her. She flashes me a grin and winks at me. I smile, giving her my everything's okay

3

face.

"It was nice meeting you both." Liar! Mini me says mocking me. Shut up, I think as I smile at them. Eric gives me a side hug, and Hawthorne drops a panty melting smile on me.

"Nice meeting you too." Now he's cute, mini me says as she perks up. When I hear the door close, I sag against the counter, wishing I could be normal. I think I'd been alone too much while I was with Dean. Maybe I took one too many blows to the head, and she is the result. Half the time I only had my inner monologue to talk to since he never let me go anywhere or see anyone after we got married. I hear a sizzle. Shit, my soup! I rush back to the stove. Didn't that just say it all? I need to get my life together. If he calls, I'll interview. If he offers me a job, I'll take it until I find something else. I'll spend the rest of my night watching the game while I work on my resume. When I'm sure it's perfect, I post it to several sites, saying a small prayer that I find something soon.

In the morning, I wake to the sound of my phone ringing. I clear my throat before I answer, not wanting to sound like I just woke despite it being ridiculously early.

"Hello." I feel good about how alert I sound.

"Madison, it's Hawthorne Price. We met last night." Did he think I forgot already? I roll my eyes. Wow, I can't believe this guy is calling me just to tell me he's not interested.

"Hawthorne, what can I do for you?" I look over at the clock. Seven in the morning. Ugh, he's a morning person. That helps make him slightly less attractive.

"I'm wondering if you are available to come in for an interview today." I perk up a little. Apparently, this was happening. I liked the thought of him holding his ground against super-bitch, I mean Irina. Then again, who knows, maybe I am just being hyper-sensitive to her.

"Uh yeah, I mean sure.. uh what time would you like to meet?" God I sound like a fumbling idiot I think as I try to get myself together.

"As soon as possible. I'm in a meeting from ten on. Can you be here in an hour?"

"I don't have a car, but I can try."

"No problem. I'll send one to pick you up."

"You don't have to do that. I can take the bus. I just need to figure out which one."

"A car will be there in forty-five minutes."

Something tells me he is a man who gets his way a lot. That makes me a little uneasy. Dean controlled everything after we got married. It got to where I barely knew him anymore.

"Okay. I'll be ready."

"Good. I look forward to it. I'll see you in an hour. Goodbye, Madison." He says before the line goes dead.

I'm honestly not even sure this is real. This is all happening so fast. Maybe I'm dreaming. Thirty minutes later, I am showered and dressed. I run around Kate's kitchen while I tried to apply some mascara and make myself a cup of coffee. I decide on heels but put flats in my bag for the bus ride home. When the car arrives, I make sure I have everything before I lock up behind myself. The car he sent is way too nice and part of me is uneasy about it. I'm not sure I fit into his world. I'm leggings and t-shirts and they are tuxedos and evening gowns. Kate fit in because to be honest she earned it. She worked hard and got herself somewhere. I stayed in our tiny town married my high school sweetheart who ended up abusing me immediately after saying "I do". Unlike her, I stayed in my bubble and didn't leave home, and it almost cost me my life. I couldn't go back. I didn't leave because I was brave, I left because Kate moved me. I stayed in the city because if I went back, Dean would find me. Somehow he'd force me to go back to him. Eventually it would lead to me dying the next time he drank too much. I had to make this work. I keep telling myself I have to make this work. Just suck it up and accept that I am here for a reason. I need to do things that make me nervous to grow into my new surroundings. Luckily for me, the driver is nice. We make small talk as he drives me across town. We pull up to a massive building that has to be a minimum of thirty floors high. It's intimidating. The driver looks at me and smiles.

"It's nice, right?"

"It's very... big."

"Well, Hawthorne has a lot of employees."

"You work for him?"

"Yep. I drive him anywhere he needs to go during the week and occasionally for personal events."

Shit, he sent his personal driver to get me. I wonder if he does this for all his potential assistants. I go to get out, and the driver scurries around as I step out. He smiles nervously, and I wonder if it worries him someone may have seen me opening my door.

"Sorry I've never had someone drive me anywhere before."

"No worries, ma'am."

"Am I crazy?" I blurt the words out without thinking.

"I'm sorry?" His brows furrow in confusion.

"I think it's obvious that I don't belong here."

"Actually, I think you'll do well here. Hawthorne likes people to just be themselves, so don't worry about fitting into a mold because this place doesn't really have one."

"Thanks. Well, wish me luck." He closes the door and smiles at me.

"Good luck, Ma'am."

"It's Maddie." I extend my hand. He smiles as he shakes it.

"I'm Ben."

"It was nice meeting you, Ben."

"The pleasure is all mine, Maddie." We smile at each other for a moment and somehow I feel better about this.

I turn and walk inside. I approach the front desk, realizing I hadn't asked what floor I needed. The man behind the desk is all kinds of intimidating until he smiles and greets me. The embroidery on his sweater says security.

"Hello. How can I help you today?"

"Hello, I am here to see Hawthorne Price."

"Sure, your name?"

"Madison Armstrong."

He smiles at me as he looks at his screen.

"Yes, Ms. Armstrong." He hands me a badge that has the word Visitor on it. I take it and clip it to the lapel of my blazer. "Take elevator one. Burt will get you where you need to go."

"Thank you." I say as I walk toward the elevators. I've never felt this out of place in my entire life.

CHAPTER TWO

Madison

Like Ben, Burt is pleasant. He smiles at me as I approach. He's ready to take me to my destination. When the elevator doors open, I step out into the nicest lobby I've ever seen. I thank Burt as the doors close. I am greeted by what I swear is an elf prince from the Lord of the Rings movies. He is tall and thin. His features are perfect. So perfect in fact it is hard to look at him. He is beautiful in an almost creepy statue like way. I force myself to focus. Do not picture him with a bow and arrow. Do not picture him with a bow and arrow. I keep repeating in my head.

"You must be Ms. Armstrong." Hmm... he doesn't sound like an Elf.

"Yes. I am." I say with a nod.

"Please have a seat. I will see if Mr. Price is ready for you." I half expect him to yell something about the hobbits being taken to Isengard and then run off to rescue them. Instead, he types something and then looks up at me and smiles. God, could he be an elf. Can he read my mind, I worry as I smile back.

"He'll be right with you." He says as the phone rings. No more movies, I chastize myself. During my recovery, I've been catching up on all things pop culture during my recovery. We watched all the Lord of the Rings and Marvel movies. We hadn't quite gotten to Harry Potter.

I nod and give him a smile. I survey my surroundings, wondering what his home must be like if his lobby at work was this nice. I bet he has a huge...

"Madison." The sound of his voice rips me from my thoughts and I can feel myself blush the moment our eyes lock. Good lord, he is handsome. He towers over me and I can tell he is all lean muscle under his fancy suit. I stand as he approaches and like yesterday, we shake hands. This time I make sure not to linger.

"Follow me."

He leads me back to his office. Just when I'm sure it can't get nicer, it does. We go through a massive door into a gigantic office that overlooks the city. He has an impressive view. He offers me a seat in the nicest black leather chair I'll ever sit in.

"Thank you for coming on such brief notice." He says as he grabs a tablet. "Would you like something to drink?" He gestures to a pitcher on the table.

"No. Thank you." I'm terrified that I will do something embarrassing like spill it all over the place. His pens are probably worth more than what is in my bank account at the moment. I cross my legs at the ankle because the skirt I borrowed from Kate's closet is a little tight on me and anything more could prove disastrous.

"Did you bring a resume?

"I did." I produce it from a folder in my bag. He looks at it and nods as he reads down the paper.

"It looks like you have a lot of experience." Shit! Here it comes. The but I don't think this is a suitable fit.

"If you don't mind my asking, why don't you want me to contact your previous employer?" He looks confused. I don't want to tell him it's because he thinks I'm dead. When Kate moved me, the officers instructed the hospital staff to tell visitors I hadn't made it.

"It's complicated." I respond thinking how that sounds like an Avril Lavigne song or a girl in a shitty relationship's Facebook status. It's hard to read his expression, but he moves on with the interview. He asks me about my skills and gives me a few scenarios asking me what I'd do. He seems very pleased with my answers, but I sense a part of him lingering on not being able to contact my former bosses. When we stand and shake hands, I'm sure I will never hear from him again. He tells me he'll be in touch. He walks me out and makes small talk as I wait for the elevator. I take one last look into his eyes as I prepare myself to never see him again. To my surprise, I am face to face with Eric as the doors open.

"Hey, Maddie."

"Eric, hi." I smile. He looks slightly less put together than usual. I wonder if he is running late after his night with Kate. Yay Kate! I cheer in my head. Hopefully, her dress survived.

"I better be going." I say stepping into the elevator. I can't resist taking one last look at Hawthorne before the doors close. "Well, I'll see you later." Eric smiles at me. I nod and let a grin spread across my face. He's a decent guy. I need to call Kate about the busses, but it would be rude to call her while I am in the elevator since I am once again in Burt's presence. I return my visitor badge and thank the guard at the desk. I step out into the bright morning sun. To my surprise, Ben is still waiting when I exit the building. He smiles at me as I walk down the steps.

"So, did you get it?" He asks a warm smile on his face as he stands by the door to the black sedan.

"I don't think so." I feel my heart sink a little.

"Don't give up hope, Maddie. I'm good at reading people and I think he could use someone like you helping him out. So where to?" I wonder what he means by someone like me, but I don't feel comfortable asking.

"Oh, I can get home on my own. I just need to know what bus to take."

"Hawthorne was very clear that I was to wait here until you finish."

"Thank you, that's very kind. I don't know the city very well yet."

"That's what I'm here for." He holds the door open for me.

We talk as he drives me back to Kate's. He has been working for Hawthorne for about five years. He had a wife, but she passed away and unfortunately, their son also passed in an accident last year. Ben is the sweetest man. I like him instantly. When we reach Kate's, I let him open my door even though it makes me feel weird. I have never been a woman of luxury and I never will be. I shake his hand and thank him for the ride. He tells me he thinks he'll be seeing me again soon. The doorman opens the door to Kate's building, and I thank Ben one last time before heading inside. My phone rings as I reach the apartment.

"Hello." I say as I open the door and step inside, locking it behind me as I kick off my heels.

"You're hired. You start tomorrow. I will send Ben to pick you up at six." I'm speechless. "Madison?"

"I'm sorry. I just… thank you." I feel a tear slip down my cheek.

"Don't thank me yet. You'll want to run away when you see the amount of emails you'll have waiting." He chuckles a little. I have to admit I like the sound.

"Six a.m. don't be late." He reminds me.

"I won't be." I'm struggling to control the full range of emotions coursing through me.

"Goodbye Madison." The way this man says my name liquifies my insides.

"Goodbye, Mr. Price." I hang up and do a dance.

I'm not sure what sealed the deal, but I'm so excited that things are finally looking up.

I call Kate. She says we have to go to dinner to celebrate. I agree because this is something to celebrate. I change into a pair of black skinny jeans and my favorite Nirvana t-shirt. I look through my clothes to see what I should wear tomorrow. I'm lost. I have to ask Kate for help because she'll know what is appropriate. I research my new employer a little before she gets home. I mean I know they're a tech company but that is about it. I pull up the company website and go to the tab that summarizes their history. As I read, I am blown away by what he has done. Apparently, he is a total genius. He went to a prestigious school and belongs to many organ-

izations. I'm intimidated. As I scroll down the lengthy list of accomplishments, it surprises me to see that he even sponsors youth
sports teams. Vaguely I think about those romance novels you
read where the guy is a mega humanitarian but likes to dominate
women. Kate and I watched the Fifty shades of Grey movies, but I
didn't get the appeal. After having a man beat me, it's kind of hard
not to go places in my head while I watch Christian get off on
spanking Ana. At first, I thought maybe Dean just wanted to play
rougher than normal, but there was no pleasure involved, only
pain existed between us. We dabbled a little before we got married,
which was how he knocked me up. We even had a safe word in case
I wanted him to stop whatever he was doing. We decided on lolli-
pop because there was never an instance where he'd be unsure
about what that meant. I wish the circumstances had been different because Jamie Dornan was hot. God, I wish I could be a normal. After what I've been through, I don't think normal is in my
future anymore. I sit there looking at the picture of Hawthorne on
the site. He is handsome. I look at those big brown eyes that
seemed so kind last night and again this morning and wonder
how he ended up with thin, blonde and bitchy. I have an hour before Kate will be home. I google Irina and hope something pops up.
Maybe a little background on her could help me handle her less
than friendly demeanor. At the very least, I was hoping to find
some common interest to make being around her bearable. Shit,
lots of stuff pops up in my search. Nothing unexpected. She is
rich, has a killer body, and the world is hers. I roll my eyes as I look
over her list of exceptional accomplishments. Oh, she is a model
turned designer. Enormous shock! She is a contributor for a fash-
ion magazine I have no interest in reading. She has a long list of
celebrity friends. Then I see them. Pictures of her and my new
boss. They are having a heated conversation as they exit the event
last night. There is an article with a headline that reads "Trouble
in Paradise" I click it because let's face it I'm curious. Apparently
thin blonde and bitchy made a scene as they were leaving last
night after having too much to drink. A picture is worth a thou-
sand words. As I study this one, I see no anger in his eyes as he es-

corts her to the car. He looks tired and worn down. I know the feeling. When Dean first started drinking too much, it was the same one I saw in the mirror. It really took a toll on me. The funny thing about alcohol is it has no prejudice. It could sneak in and take hold of you no matter your social or economic status. I need to stop being a stalker. I close out my screen feeling like I violated him. Kate arrives at her usual time and changes. We settle on a small pizza joint a few blocks away. While we walk, she tells me all about her night. Apparently, Eric made good on the promise he whispered in her ear. She told me she took care of the dress and made sure she draped it on a chair. Part of me wants to ask about the report I saw but I don't want Kate reading into my curiosity.

"So, how was rubbing elbows with the rich and famous?"

"It was fun until Irina decided it wasn't. She made a scene and when Hawthorne wanted to leave, it escalated." She shakes her head and rolls her eyes.

"I don't think we should talk about it. It might not be something I need to know about my new boss."

"Well, you won't be seeing much of her. I think they called it off."

"Is it bad that I don't feel bad about that?" I make a face.

"Oh my God! Do you have a crush on your new boss already?"

"What? No! That chick was a total bitch to me and if I never see her again, I won't feel bad. Actually, it was the one thing I worried about with this entire thing."

"Wait what happened last night?"

"She was rude and dismissive. I'm sure the thought of touching me bothered her. I mean, she literally left me hanging when I offered her my hand. I think someone needs to tell her you can't catch poor."

"That bitch! If I had known I would have tripped her on the step and repeat or at least spilled a drink on her by accident." She smirks.

I laugh because as petty as it is, she always has my back. I love that her success never changed her. She is still that girl who would stick by me no matter what.

"So, you mean to tell me you're not even a little attracted to Hawthorne?"

"He's my new boss, Kate. I am not going there. Besides, I'm not exactly free to start anything I'm still married. Beyond the married thing I just don't know if I can let someone in that way."

"I'm taking that as yes! Maddie I know dating isn't on your mind because of everything that's happened but if the opportunity arises, you shouldn't feel obligated to a marriage that ended."

I knew she wouldn't drop it if I didn't just give in and admit that he was attractive.

"He's cute. Even if he wasn't my boss, I'm not exactly in the mind-set to start something. I need to wrap up the past before I can move forward."

Kate drops it because she's satisfied with my admission, and we finish dinner. Dating may not be something that comes easily to me. Kate is the only person I can stand to have touch me. She held me for hours while I cried, and some nights even fell asleep in the hospital bed next to me. She's been my light in the dark. I worry that my being here is hindering her and Eric from being together more. At dinner when I bring up apartment hunting, she doesn't seem too thrilled about me moving out. She even suggests that we get a bigger place together. I ask her about moving in with Eric, and she says she isn't sure if they are that serious yet. He's been a little distant, and she isn't sure how she feels about him. I guess only time would tell about Eric, but I hope he is more into Kate than she realizes. She should be with someone who will love her the way she deserves. As I attempt to sleep and fail, I think about what my life will be like here in the city. I should be a glass half full person, but I am always waiting for the other shoe to drop. Dean is still out there. For all I know, he might already know where I am now that we continued the divorce proceedings. I'm always looking over my shoulder. I don't want to live in fear. After losing my baby and a few weeks of my memory, I have an excellent reason. I need to learn how to defend myself. Maybe I could find a self-defense course or a boxing class here. I won't be the next Rocky Balboa, but I want to know how to get out of a dangerous situation. I should take Kate with me since I may have inadvertently put her in danger. I figure I'll sleep on it and ask her about it tomorrow. I'm so lost and for the first time in a long time I pray. Not to God, but to Gram. I ask for her guidance and her strength. I really could use a guardian angel right now.

The next morning, just as Hawthorne promised, Ben is out front at six sharp, standing there with an enormous grin on his face.

"Good morning." He beams.

"Good morning, Ben." A smile spreads across my face.

He opens the door, and I get in. It surprises me to see Hawthorne sitting there already on a call. Our eyes lock and I feel my cheeks flush when he smiles at me. God, he smells good. I have to get this attraction under control if I plan on staying his assistant. I can't let him see how he affects me. I don't know him and I won't become his next plaything. I am determined to never be at any man's mercy again.

"Listen, I'll call you back when I get to the office." He ends the call and looks over at me. "Good morning." He flashes me a killer smile. I feel the familiar heat return to my cheeks. "Good morning." I busy myself with buckling my seatbelt. It gives me a much-needed excuse to look away.

"So, I thought we would stop and grab some coffee on the way in. I'll give you a rundown on what I'll need from you daily."

"Sounds good." I steady myself before I look over at him. "You might need to take notes." "I didn't bring a pad." I wince at my rookie mistake. I should have known he'd want to get right down to it. He looks at me like I have three heads. "A pad!" The tone of his voice is enough to make my eyes sting with embarrassment. "Just use your phone." I feel my cheeks blaze as I look down at my fingers.

"I can't."

"Why not?" He frowns. "Notes is there for a reason if you don't like notes there are other apps." I can't tell what the look on his face means, but I honestly think I'm about to get fired. I hadn't even gotten to the office yet.

"Look, I need someone who will take this seriously." He exhales his frustration. I can tell he's irritated.

"I am. I swear." I feel my eyes get glossy. "I'll do my best to remember what you say, and I will make sure I have a planner or a pad by tomorrow."

"Give me your phone. I'll show you how to use it and start entering your email and all my contact info." He's irritated as he holds his hand out. "I know what notes is and I know how to use it." I say a little more defensive than I mean to sound. I blink my eyes a few times, hoping to keep tears of embarrassment from running down my face. I reach in my purse and pull out my phone. I slip it into his hand and look anywhere but at him.

"What is this?" he holds it up.

"My phone." I feel myself shrinking in the seat beside him. I force myself to look at him.

"God, they still make these?" He says examining my phone like it is an ancient relic. That's it! I think as I contemplate how bad it would be to tell him off.

"Yeah, I know it's bad." I reign in my anger after deciding that a paycheck is more important than my pride right now.

"I'll get a smartphone when I get my first paycheck. I promise it's just without a job it was a luxury not a necessity." He hands me my phone back, and I wish I could die or slap him. The latter more than the former. Not everyone has money like he does. I've become good at masking what I feel on the outside mostly but inside I'm a mess. He moves on to what my typical day will be like, and I am glad that it is an independent work environment. I need to know his every move. I need to ensure meeting and conference rooms and resources are ready as he needs them. He needs me to tend to the fine details. Ironically, my old life has set me up to be the perfect assistant. After Dean and I married, he became controlling and demanding. Before I said I do, he never laid a hand on me. Once I uttered those words, I became property. It started off slow, mostly verbal insults and him being rough physically with me. The first time he slapped me, I remember standing there in disbelief. The shock and the shame kept me silent. I didn't tell anyone, not even Kate, not that there was anyone else to tell. She is my only close friend, I didn't have parents. The thought of telling my Gram that my husband hit me was unbearable. Afterwards he never told me he was sorry or ashamed or that it would never happen again. It was clear he wasn't sorry or ashamed, and if I didn't do what he wanted, it would happen again. I began trying to expect what his mood might be and get ahead of it. The next time he hit me, he used his fists. It progressed until I could no longer hide it. I always had bruises where no one could see them when he finished. Eventually he stopped caring about who could see. The first severe beating resulted from his dinner being cold. He didn't care that his being over an hour late from work was the reason. I remember wanting to die just so I'd stop feeling. I had trouble dressing myself for a week afterward and had to wear cover up to hide my black eye and bruised cheek. I'm pulled from my thoughts when we stop in front of a small café. It surprises me because he seems like he'd be a Starbucks kind of guy.

"Come on." He holds his hand out to me as Ben opens the door. He helps me out of the car. I do everything possible to avoid eye contact. The warmth of his hand wrapped around mine sends a tingle up my arm.

"We'll stop here in the mornings. I'd like you to pre-order so it's ready when we get here. We'll get this phone situation taken care of when we get to the office. The benefit of working for me means you get cool gadgets." I look down, hoping he doesn't notice the lingering tears in my eyes. He gives me a reassuring smile and I wonder if he feels bad about making fun of my phone. As we wait in line, a girl at the counter gives him googly eyes. Not that I blame her. He is very attractive. When it is time to take his order, another girl comes over, stepping in.

"Hey Hawthorne, a new assistant?" She smiles at me. She is unfazed by him and it makes me curious if the reason is that she's been there and done that.

"Yeah, Tris, this is Madison." She gives me a subtle once over and smiles.

"Nice to meet you, Madison."

"Nice to meet you too." I smile.

"So, what will it be?" She looks at me.

"Oh, I'm good."

"Oh, no, are you a morning person?" Her face twists in disgust.

"Not really. I already had a cup before I left this morning."

"Even worse, she's a one cup a day person." She laughs. "You'll never last around this one if you don't like coffee as much as he does."

"All right, leave her alone Tris. I don't need you telling her all my awful habits on the first day. I don't want her running."

She raises her hands up in surrender as she winks at me. Something tells me Tris and I could be friends.

"Seriously, Madison, order something because there aren't any of those K-cups left at the office. My assistant usually orders them, and she quit last minute. Let's just say, I am definitely out."

"Okay." I say in surrender.

"I'll have a tall White Chocolate Mocha."

"Venti." Hawthorne says as he smiles. "She'll need it." Tris responds as she goes about working her magic.

When I go to pay, I swear his eyes nearly pop out of his head and roll across the counter. Tris laughs and shakes her head.

"You guys have an expense account with us so anytime you come in you just scan the barcode for the company and this guy foots the bill."

I nod as he looks around, almost as if to make sure no one saw me attempt to pay. When our order is ready, we say goodbye to Tris before leaving. She waves at us as we make our way out. He opens the door for me, and I like the fact that he is old school. I remind myself not to get too comfortable with him. He is my boss but more than that he is a man and I am a woman. I don't want people getting the wrong idea. We spend the ride to the office talking about the company. It's nice to forget about everything except what's happening right now. All the stuff with Dean, losing the baby and trying to figure out how I move on from something like this. Dealing with the memory gaps has been exhausting. I get to put it aside for now because it'll still be there later when I got home. While I'm working, I get to be someone else. I get to be confident and feel like I have control versus the reality I live outside of the office. It feels good. I think I will like it here. The best part is no one knows what happened to me. Here I'm just Madison.

Later that night, I run through my day with Kate over some Chinese takeout. It really is good to be doing something with my degree. My hard work might finally pay off. I almost passed out when I saw what I would be making. It is nice to know that I should be able to get an apartment soon and give Kate her space back. My job came with all kinds of new goodies. Hawthorne is right, working for a tech company has its perks. I now have a very nice, very expensive laptop and the newest phone available. I need to make a plan. I look at apartments for rent. I also look at bus routes because I need to learn how to get around on my own. Just my second day and I've accomplished so much in a few hours. My heart sinks when I notice a few of the women from accounting whispering in the break room. I'm minding my business, just heating leftovers from last night. If they see me driving into work with the boss every morning, people would undoubtably think the worst. I had to figure out my way into work alone. Then I had to tell him I could do this on my own. After searching the bus routes, I figured out that it would take two busses to get from Kate's to the office. That isn't too bad. Now to text him and tell him I wouldn't need a ride in the morning. I type and erase, then re-type and erase and do it all over again. When I have finally crafted a message that seems acceptable, I hit send and hold my breath.

He reads it instantly, which makes me wonder if he just has that damn phone connected to him all day. I laugh as I picture him responding to texts in his sleep. That doesn't help because now I am thinking about what he wears to bed. I have to stop this.

Me: Hi, sorry to bother you. I just wanted to thank you for the ride today. I researched the bus schedule, so I am all good for tomorrow.

Hawthorne: You're welcome, but I would really prefer it if you ride with me.

Someone doesn't enjoy hearing no, I think as I look at my phone.

Me: I just think it would be better if I wasn't riding into work with my boss every morning.

Hawthorne: Did I do something?

Me: No. You're great!

Hawthorne: So, what's the problem?

Ugh, how could I explain this without telling him what happened?

Me: I just don't want people getting the wrong impression and besides I need to learn my way around the city on my own.

Hawthorne: Did something happen?

Me: No. I just don't want to take advantage of your kindness.

Hawthorne: I never do things I don't want to do. I'm not someone who gets taken advantage of.

Me: I know.

Hawthorne: Good! Then I will see you in the morning?

Me: Okay.

I felt like an idiot for even bringing this up. Man, first day on the job and I was already a paranoid mess. The stress of everything that I have been dealing with had to be getting to me because normally I wouldn't have given two shits about the whispering in the break room. I had gotten used to people whispering whether it was in high school about me and Kate or around town when I started showing up in public with black eyes and busted lips. Everyone always had an opinion my entire life. As I go to bed, I decide that first chance I got, I should find someone to talk to. I need to get this mess in my head figured out. I don't want to lay anymore of this on Kate. I also want to look for a self-defense class. If I move out and start getting around the city alone, I need to be ready in case my past comes crashing down on me. As much as I like Hawthorne, I need to be careful around him. He is charming and powerful. I need to remember that. It's a dangerous combination. The ride thing should have been a simple thanks but I can manage and it turned into me still riding with him and then feeling guilty that I bothered him. I need to be more assertive. I can't believe how I've changed. I used to be that girl calling plays to win the game. The one who wasn't afraid of everything. I miss the person I was so much. Life used to be simple. I was in control and now I'm a mess.

CHAPTER THREE

Hawthorne

My phone dings, I'm a little annoyed because it's most likely Irina again. After the shit she pulled at the Gala, I ended it. Petty jealousy from time to time was one thing, but she took it too far that night. The public disaster was the last straw for me. I won't be with someone I can't trust. The stuff that happened with my last assistant was crazy. When I found out the way Irina had been treating Hailey, I was furious. How hadn't I noticed? Even though I am a busy person, I should have seen the changes in Hailey. Towards the end she wouldn't look at me. Maybe she thought I was okay with Irina's behavior. I mean, she didn't even ask for a letter of recommendation when she told me she was quitting. After Irina's reaction to Madison, I was certain I would pay for lingering when I shook her hand. That minor thing caused the breakdown at the Gala. She freaked out on me over a handshake that lingered. I read the message ready to get whatever argument she deems necessary over with now. It's ironic she is the cheater and yet I'm the one always being accused. To my surprise, the text is from Madison. She's declining a ride to work. I see red as I read it. This can't be happening again. I wonder if Irina is making good on her threat to make my life hell. For a beautiful, successful woman, she's the most insecure person I've ever met. It is her most unattractive feature. I sympathized with her in the beginning. At first, no matter how successful I became or how much money I had, I was still that tall nerd from high school on the inside. Moving on means you have to move past who you were. For me, Madison's level of comfort with herself is a major turn on. It's something I admire the most about her. She didn't seem nervous at all as Eric introduced her to us. I think it's what set Irina off to begin with. Madison didn't seem to care that she was in leggings and a t-shirt with her hair in a messy bun while being introduced to one of the most powerful men in the city. It pissed her off when I held her gaze and her hand a little longer than I should have. Something about Madison just sucks me in. It's only been a few days and I can't stop thinking about her. I don't want her enduring Irina's wrath because of me. Irina would chew her up and spit her out in the public eye if she felt like it. She knows how to spin a story and play the press. I planned on keeping this professional as I always did with all my assistants, even after I checked into her past. What my private security found is very dark and scary. The kind of things I couldn't get passed. Things that would haunt my thoughts. The nagging need to keep her safe from what is lurking in the shadows is taking over me. I know I shouldn't but after seeing everything there is no going back. I have a multitude of police reports and a restraining order that hadn't been enough to keep her safe in my inbox. My head spins while I read through them. I don't want her out there alone. It's crazy how you can meet someone take one look in their eyes and feel more in that moments time then in two years with someone else. I never should have hired her, especially because of how attracted I am to her. Me being her boss complicates things. The only way to keep her safe is to keep her close. I can't let Irina ruin this second chance for her. If anyone has an opinion on me hiring Maddie, they can take it up with me. I can tell from her texts something happened but I would get nothing out of her. I'm able to convince her to stick with our current plan of driving together. Madison doesn't strike me as someone looking to be taken care of. I have no right to feel this protective of her or to insert myself into her life the way I already have but there's no stopping this now. Until I knew if this thing that I feel is real I plan on doing everything I can to find her ex. I need to make sure that he will not be a problem for her. My email alert pings. Another set of files comes through these are on the ex. The mug shots from his arrests are included. He has dirty blonde hair and bright blue eyes. The kind girls get all googly eyed for. He looks like the smug guys I hated growing up . The guys who humiliated me every chance they got just to feel better about themselves. No doubt he played sports and thought he was a big shot because he could swing a stick and hit a ball. I want to break his perfect nose. God knows if I ever get the chance I will. I'm not that skinny kid anymore. I made sure that I would never be the least powerful man in a room again. Before I dig too deep into the files my door-bell rings. I already know who it is. I am not in the mood for this interruption. I shut the door to my office. There is no need for any-one least of all Irina to see what I'm working on. The sooner I an-swer the sooner I can get this over with. As I expect Irina is stand-ing there. She's pissed as she barges her way into my place.

"You owe me an explanation." She says still facing away from me, her hands on her hips.

"I don't owe you shit." I fold my arms as I narrow my eyes at her.

"You hired her! I can't believe you would do that! Did you hire her to get back at me? Are you already fucking her?"

"I hired her because thanks to you I needed a new assistant. Not that it's any of your business, but no, I am not fucking her! I don't get it you cheat on me and I am the one on trial here." I scoff.

"We moved past it." Her voice softens, and she turns, swatting her hand through the air.

"No! You moved past it. I have very much been living in it since I found out. It was just a matter of time before I admitted that I can't move past it." I hear my phone ding. I immediately wonder if it is Madison.

"So, you were just stringing me along?" She walks toward me slowly unbuttoning her coat to reveal the lingerie she has on underneath. Is she trying to seduce me?

"I didn't string you along. I was trying to decide if I loved you enough that I could get past it." She steps up against my body and I shake my head as I look away.

"Hawthorne, I know you still love me?" Her ego is out of control.

Her hand slides down my stomach to my crotch and her brow furrows in anger at my complete lack of arousal.

"I don't. I can't trust you." I remove her hands from my body.

"That's it you move on without so much as a tear and I'm supposed to just get over it? Jesus, did you ever love me?" Her eyes water, but I know it's all an act. She put on quite the show when I found out about her extracurricular activities. This isn't the first time I have witnessed her ability to cry on command.

"I did, but it became very clear that nothing would ever be enough for you. You cheating only confirmed that."

"I guess we have nothing else to say." She straightens and I can see her defenses go up as if they were a physical wall.

"I guess we don't. I don't expect you to be dropping by the office or here unannounced again. I don't want you bothering Madison either. She isn't your concern, and she has absolutely nothing to do with me ending this. It was just a matter of time before we ended up here."

She reaches out, placing her hands on my chest. I look down at her and she tips up on her toes and kisses me softly on the lips. I don't kiss her back. I feel nothing. No heartache, not even an ounce of lust. I truly have moved on. It started when she cheated, and now I know I did the right thing when I cut ties. She steps back and takes one last look up at me. She leaves without another word. I lock the door behind her and immediately go see who texted me. It isn't Madison. It's my private security telling me he sent me more files and if he finds anything more, he will forward it to me. I thank him and go back into my office. I can't bear looking at that asshole's face on my monitor. I close it and look through the other attachments. That's when I see that there are more photos. I click on the first one and Madison's bruised face pops up on my screen. Her cheek looks bruised. She looks worn down and scared. Vomit rises in my throat. The next series of photos shows a slow progression of the abuse. The next one has her sporting a black eye and a busted lip. The one after that shows choke marks on her neck and

25

the last one shows bruises all over her side and back. I stop, unable to stomach any more. All I know is she would never have another bruise or busted lip at the hands of this asshole or any man ever again if I have anything to say about it. I shut things down and get ready for bed because I have a day of meetings ahead of me. I skip dinner. My stomach can't handle it after those photos, my appetite is non existent. I need to get a few hours of sleep. Easier said than done because when I close my eyes all I can see is her bruised face. Those pained eyes full of shame because of what that asshole did to her.

The next morning, I get ready and meet Ben outside. As usual, he's waiting and chipper. He's happy he'll get to see Madison again. After our first meeting, he had taken an unusual liking to her. That night when he drives me home, he asks if he'll have the pleasure of seeing her again. I tell him we'll be picking her up in the morning and a slow smile spreads across his face. He knows it's unusual that we are picking her up on the way to the office. Something tells me this is already a thing for him. He told me Irina wasn't an excellent fit when she and I first had problems. Even though he works for me, he is family. His son and I grew up together and when he passed away, I tried to do my best to keep the family whole. His son's widow works for me, and I made sure the child he left behind has everything he could need. I even sponsor his youth sports teams and coach them when I can. Ben is the closest thing I have to a father. When he started getting older, he came to work for me because he refused to retire. Letting me take care of him wasn't an option he'd even consider. Him being my driver is the happy medium we'd come to when he needed to slow down a bit.

Madison is ready and waiting when we arrive. She looks amazing and smells even better. It's something I try hard not to notice as we drive. She seems a little distracted on the drive to the coffee shop. Even though I barely know her, I can tell she is wrestling with something.

"Everything okay?"

"I just want to say I'm sorry about last night. I didn't mean to come off unappreciative or anything. I really appreciate this job and your kindness."

"No worries. Look if anyone gives you any trouble just promise you'll let me know. I should probably tell you the reason my last assistant quit. My ex Irina had it in her head that I was having an affair with my last assistant, Hailey. I wasn't. I'm not that guy. She did everything she could to make Hailey's life hell. I didn't pick up on what was happening until it was too late. She ended up quitting before I could do anything about it." She sits there with a stunned look on her face. I wonder if I've said too much. A little less truth might have been better, but I don't want to have this be something she hears from someone else.

"I'm sorry."

"Don't be. I got this great new assistant, so things are looking up."

Her answering laugh is something I could listen to on repeat and never tire of. The smile is on a whole other level. How any man could bring himself to hurt her is beyond me. Slowly we get to know each other day by day. These rides give us some informal time to talk. I take every opportunity I can to learn something about her. I learn the simple things. It starts with small stuff like her favorite color. It's blue. It's a color I now wear a little more than I used to. We go on like this for a few months and I have to say I am really enjoying the time we spend together on the way to work. I like her. I wonder if she feels the same way.

I'm hard at work and everything seems handled so I decide maybe today is the day I grow a pair and ask her to lunch. I made a serious dent in my workload for the day. By lunch, I am starving and craving Mexican food. I poke my head out of the office to see if Madison is on the phone. She isn't, so it's now or never. I shouldn't, but I can't help myself, I like her. I call over for her, asking her to come into my office. She grabs her tablet and smiles at me as she stands. I have my back to her when she closes the door. I'm nervous. I should have put my suit jacket back on or at least rolled my sleeves down. I'm hate that I look sloppy. I sit on the edge of my desk. I'm stalling because I'm nervous. I can do this! I haven't been this nervous in a very long time. I practiced this in my head a million times. I can do this, I repeat in my head. Something flickers in her eyes as she looks at me. She quickly averts her gaze and blushes as she clears her throat. My internal struggle is making this awkward. I wish I had some insight into what she is thinking. If my fly is down, I will die. I look down, a quick check tells me I'm all good. Is she staring at my tattoos? I knew I should have covered up.

"Madison." I say getting her attention.

She clears her throat again and shakes herself a little. I wonder if they turn her on or off.

"Yes, Mr. Price." The way she says my name has me hoping the former is more on the mark.

"Are you hungry, Madison?" I ask as I smile at the thought of her being turned on by me.

"I'm sorry?" She asks looking up at me confused. Her cheeks are slightly flush.

"I am wondering if you want to get lunch?"

"Sure, I can go get your lunch." This is not going the way I planned.

"No, I meant go to lunch with me."

Her eyes dart between my eyes and my arms. Then they dropped to the floor as if she's having an internal struggle, but she settles on a decision.

"I ... bring... lunch." She stammers.

"Right." The sting of her rejection is painful. "If only I could get organized like you are. I'll be back in an hour. Hold my calls." My hope deflates. With every second that passes, I feel more like that tall skinny nerd from high school. She's avoiding eye contact and I hate the thought of me being the reason she's uncomfortable.

"Okay. Will that be all?" She practically darts up from the chair she's in.

"Yes, thank you."

She scurries out as if she can't wait to get away from me. Shit, did I come on too strong? Maybe I read everything all wrong. When I leave to get lunch and clear my head, Madison isn't at her desk. She's probably waiting until I leave to come out of hiding. I need to fill my stomach and check on my ego because it's hurting right now. How could I be so stupid? I mean, she seems to like me. No matter how old or successful I become in business, my personal life is always a mess. Maddie never would have even looked at me in high school. I know from our conversations she was part of the sports crowd back then, I'm guessing that's how she met the all-American wife beater. I just wish she'd let me in, maybe even give me a chance to show her that something different is out there. Someone who would treat her better.

CHAPTER FOUR

Madison

I escape to the bathroom because I need to breathe. I mean, did I just ogle my boss? One look at those muscular arms all tatted up, and I was wetter than I had ever been in my entire life. I need to be careful because this job is the most important thing I have going right now. This has to work. I stand there with my back against the stall when I hear two women come in. They are mid conversation.

"Did you see her outfit today? She is man hunting. Her tight skirt and that blouse shows so much cleavage. I heard she is in his office a lot."

"What a slut! Not that I blame her, he is hot and rich!" One of them giggles.

"I hear she rides to work with him."

"I bet Madison's riding him after work too."

"You can tell she's a total whore. She plays sweet an innocent, but I bet she's on her knees half the day in his office."

I want to bust out of there and slap a bitch, but it's imperative that I keep my composure because that would get me fired and possibly arrested. It's weird, but I haven't felt this aggressive since I played hockey. In those days, I would have pulled my gloves off and thrown a blow or two. Maybe I was getting back to who I was before my life went to shit. I wasn't just angry about them calling me a slut. I was mad that they were assuming Hawthorne was that kind of guy. I had to stay put. I needed this job. I was so damn close to getting things wrapped up with the divorce and getting an apartment so Kate could get her life back to normal. A few minutes later the door opened again and the two of them shuffled their way on out. Cackling like the bitches they were. I felt the tears stinging my eyes as I exited the stall. I'm angry because I now know there's really no safe place anymore. Stop this! I tell myself. You need to splash some water on your face and get back out there. I mean seriously I was a few months in I couldn't give up. That would be like me blowing my shot at a goal in the third period. Besides, I like my job. Hawthorne is a great boss. As I dry my face, the woman from HR walks in. She smiles at me and then her smile fades a little.

"Everything okay?" She asks as I finish drying my face.

"Yes." I say, forcing a smile.

"Madison, if you need to talk, you remember where my office is right?"

I nod and smile. She takes one last look at me before she goes into a stall. I toss the paper towel and do a once over before going back to my desk. Thankfully, Hawthorne already left. If he saw me like this, he'd probably demand to know what happened. God, he was perfect. It was so never going to happen with him. I mean, he's nice to everyone. He treats everyone with respect, but someone like him would never go for someone like me. I'm sure once he found out about Dean and saw the remnants he left on my skin, Hawthorne wouldn't want me that way. This thing with him was like a schoolgirl crush. I just need to get over it.

"Did you want to go to lunch now?" I jump because I'm unaware anyone had approached. Theo, AKA Legolas snuck up on me. This isn't the first time he's used his elf ninja skills on me.

"Sorry. I didn't mean to startle you." He's accessing me in some weird way.

"It's okay. I'm just lost in my head. Go ahead, I'm not hungry yet."

"Everything okay?" Oh, dear lord, was that an actual emotion coming across his face?

"Yeah, I Um…" I clear my throat a little. "I'm I taking a late lunch.

It's kind of crowded in there."

He makes a face as he nods. He doesn't linger something I appreciate. I should get my mind off what I know is being said about me and just focus on work. Hawthorne doesn't make it back before Theo, so when I leave for lunch he will probably return and be in his office for the rest of the afternoon. Bonus! I probably won't have the chance to embarrass myself for a while. Thank God! After most of the crowd clears, I go into the break room and warm up my food. I eat alone. It's probably best because I don't know who I can trust around here. When I return to my desk, I am summoned to HR. Immediately a pit forms in my stomach. Burt smiles at me as I step into the elevator. He asks where I am going. I tell him human resources and force a smile. I take a breath, hoping to quiet the storm happening inside of me. When the elevator stops the doors open, Burt looks over at me. I smile and thank him as I force myself out and over to their front desk operator. She smiles at me and tells me to go back to the conference room, that they're ready for me and vaguely I wonder who they are. I am shocked to see not only the head of HR but Eric and Hawthorne sitting at the table. I feel myself swallow hard as I step in and close the door behind me. Shit, am I being fired? Don't cry, don't cry, I repeat in my head as I try to play it cool. I'm offered a seat and I take it. I sit, putting my hands in my lap. It's my best attempt at not fidgeting.

"Madison, I just wanted to check in. I asked Hawthorne and Eric to sit in so that everyone was privy to this conversation. Someone came to me earlier with a concern. They mentioned something about seeing you upset today." Eric's head drops a little as he exhales, and I wonder if he's angry. Vaguely, I'm aware of Hawthorne's jaw clenching at my other side. My eyes drop only for a moment and then I force myself to look up. I could do this. I'm good at giving people the truth they need.

"I'm not sure what you're talking about."

"Look Madison I know this job is important to you but if something happened that made you uncomfortable you need to tell someone. We have a policy about these things and if someone crossed a line no matter who it is, we need to know. There will be no retaliation." She gives a brief look up at Hawthorne and he nods his head.

"No line crossing going on here." I force a smile. It's my "everything's all good here officer" face, the one I would use after someone reported hearing banging and shouting coming from the apartment Dean and I lived in.

"Do you mind me asking what upset you. When I ran into you earlier in the restroom, you looked like you had been crying." I notice Hawthorne stiffen a little.

"Oh." I say, feigning embarrassment. "I um... was doing something, and I remembered something my gram used to say. I lost her less than a year ago and I needed to take a minute. We were close. She raised me when my parents died."

"I'm so sorry. I didn't mean to read into it. I just had to check in and make sure everything was okay."

"I understand. I thank you for your concern."

Eric smiles over at me, but it doesn't reach his eyes. He knows that I'm lying, I can sense it. His face reminds me of the officers who didn't believe me when I said the noise was a movie or the TV. Hawthorne doesn't look at me, and I wonder what he's thinking. After making sure that I know I should report anything that feels inappropriate to HR directly or go to Eric or Hawthorne, I am relieved to go back to my work. I'm not sure what to think as I ascend back to where I belong. Theo looks at me as I exit the elevator. He's accessing me in some weird elf prince way that I really don't have the energy to decipher right now. I honestly can't tell if he likes me or hates me half the time. I take a seat at my desk and rub the center of my forehead, trying to ward off the headache that's starting to set in. I hear the elevator open and the sound of Hawthorne's assertive footsteps heading my way. He looks upset.

"Please join me in my office." His lack of eye contact has me worried.

I stand and follow him. He doesn't face me as he paces the floor in front of the window. I stall by the door.

"Close the door and have a seat." He stops moving and takes a deep breath. I do what he asks and brace myself as I sit. I can tell he's angry.

"You want to tell me why you lied in there?" He turns, pegging me with the heat of his angry eyes.

"I don't know what you're talking about?" I wince. Shit, this is turning into another one of those migraines I'd been getting since I left the hospital.

"I don't enjoy getting calls during my lunch saying that they saw my assistant crying in the bathroom. Was it me? Did I do something wrong?"

"No. Why would you think it had to do with you?" He seems to soften a bit. Now he's avoiding my gaze.

"I like you, Madison. I don't want anyone that includes myself crossing any lines with you. You are safe here and if anyone even me is doing something that bothers you to the extent of you crying in the bathroom I need to know. My last assistant left because she didn't feel safe here. I failed her. I won't fail you too. I can't fail you." His admission strains his voice.

Shit, he knew. I thought.

"Who told you? Eric?" I'm too distracted by the throbbing in my head to express the anger swirling inside my head.

The way he looks at me, the pity in his eyes makes me angry.

"I have a security team that digs into my potential assistants. I need to know I can trust you fully."

"Let me guess, me telling you I didn't want you to contact my last employer was me waving a big red flag." I close my eyes, rubbing the spot between them. I need to suppress my rage and slow this goddamn migraine down.

"Yes." He puts his palms on his desk and hangs his head.

"I want to see what you have."

His head bolts up. "I don't have it here it's on my personal computer at home."

"Well, I want to see it. It'd be nice to know what information you bought about me."

"Okay. Look, I'm sorry."

"Don't say you're sorry we both know you'd do it again."

I stand and go to the door. I need to get my medicine and quick before this thing ends up being a full-blown nightmare.

"Please don't quit."

"I can't afford to quit. I need this job, but I am not happy. You finding out about my private life like this..." I exhaled. "I'm embarrassed and to be honest, I feel violated."

"Madison, I didn't do this to hurt you or embarrass you."

I open the door.

"I know but it doesn't change the fact that you did." I shut the door softly behind me. I go to my desk, taking my migraine medicine out of my purse. I need to get ahead of this thing otherwise it will wreck me. Migraines were one of the lovely after effects of being beaten half to death. I go to the break room to grab a cup of water. When I return to my desk, I try my hardest to stay calm. I don't need this thing getting worse. When our day is over we ride down in the elevator in uncomfortable silence. I don't look at him and he doesn't make small talk as he normally would. We exit the building and for the first time I don't care who might see. After tonight it might be the last time that I ever step foot on this property. I've had too much time to sit and stew about this, which hasn't helped my migraine in the least. Thank God this car has tinted windows. I quickly realize we are not going toward Kate's place.

"Where are we going?"

"My place you said you wanted to see your file."

"Can't you just bring your laptop into work?" I groan as I rub my forehead, wishing the pain would just subside a little.

35

"It's not a laptop my home system is more extensive and I can't transport it."

"Fine, let's get this over with" I bite out. The look on his face makes me feel like a bitch, but then I remind myself that I was the one who wronged. I don't look at him because I'm sitting here feeling bad for him when I should be angry. Doesn't that just say it all? I'm reminded of how I started defending Dean's behavior even after he started hurting me.

"I didn't do this to violate your privacy but when your name began appearing in police reports, I needed to know if you were a risk."

"I don't mean to be rude, but can we just drive in silence? I have been getting these migraines since... well for a while and if I sit in darkened silence for a while it helps once I see auras I'm screwed. It gets ugly fast after that."

"Sorry." He silences his phone as it rings and rests his head back on the seat.

I close my eyes, exhale and do the same. I'm feeling a little better by the time we got to his place. He lives in the nicest part of town. No surprise there. Ben pulls into a parking garage and lets us out by an elevator. He leads me up to his place, which is exactly what I expect. Everything is immaculate and top of the line. It's a little obnoxious. He tells me I can set my things down on the couch. Immediately I think of how out of place my things are here, how out of place I am here. I was stupid to entertain being happy working for him. He gestures toward the hallway. I follow him and wonder if he can hear how hard my heart is thumping. He opens the way into the most intense office I had ever seen. There is a huge glass monitor on the wall that makes me wonder if I'm working for a real-life Tony Stark. The tech at the office was nice, but this is some next level stuff. Even I knew that. The monitor came to life with a touch of his hand and he had to look at the camera to unlock it. He hits a few things and files pop up on the screen. As I looked at every police report, evidence photo and mug shot that pops up, I am overwhelmed by what I let

Dean do to me. It's not so much that he did it, but that I let it happen. The black eyes, the busted lips, the bruises and injuries are all there. I am literally face to face with my past. I don't recognize the person I had become. As I look from photo to photo, seeing the progression of the abuse and the toll it took on me, I feel my head pounding and my chest aching for what I became. I don't notice the tears falling down my cheeks until he says my name. I look at him. He is blurry to my teary eyes.

"I'm sorry, Madison. You deserve better than this." I can tell he is unsure of how to comfort me.

"If I'm honest, there is so much more than what you even have here. I don't know how I let this happen." I'm ashamed and unable to look him in the eyes. This is too much for me to process. Suddenly I feel sick.

"Can I use your bathroom?" I'm trying to breathe through the vomit creeping up my throat.

"Sure. It's out and to the right." His eyes widen as I run out.

I make it in time to empty the contents of my stomach in his toilet. He comes up behind me and holds my hair as the second wave hits. I don't have time to deal with being mortified right now. I am no longer in control of this thing.

CHAPTER FIVE

Hawthorne

I watch the color drain from Madison's face as she turns and bolts out of the room. I follow her because she looks like she'll be sick. She falls to her knees, vomiting once she reaches the toilet. I'm about to turn on the light, but I remember what she said about the light and her migraine. The darkness might also save her further embarrassment. I have to comfort her, I can't stop myself. I walk up behind her and gather her hair to hold it back. She grips the toilet and gives it hell again. Things settle. She flushes and sits back, bracing herself for another wave as she takes deep breaths.

"I'm sorry. Once these things start, I can't control it."

"Don't apologize, just let me help you." She nods, taking a deep breath.

"Do you want to brush your teeth?"

She sighs. "That'd be heaven."

Going to the sink, I grab a fresh toothbrush from the drawer and squeeze some toothpaste on it. She sits on the edge of the tub and brushes. She needs to rinse, so I help brace her as she stands at the sink.

"Call Kate. I can't get home by myself." She says as she sways a little. "I do not want Ben seeing me throw up. I have a one guy seeing me vomit a day limit." At least she still has a sense of humor. It gives me hope that she might not hate me.

"I'm not sending you out there like this. You're staying here."

She looks up like she wants to argue, but she says nothing. She knows she won't make it home without something bad happening on the way.

"I need to get you into bed." She lifts her head her eyes widen as if she's about to argue.

"You need to rest." Picking her up, I carry her into my bedroom. I'm surprised that she doesn't fight me.

"I can rest on the couch." She says as I set her on the bed.

"Believe me, you don't want to sleep there your back will hurt for a week."

"Why would you pick something uncomfortable?" Her brow furrows I'm not sure if it's because of the migraine or confusion.

"It wasn't my first pick." I don't tell her I wanted something softer, but Irina forced me into this one. She had a look in mind for the place. I hate that couch. Come to think of it, I hate a lot of the stuff she helped me pick. That is the first red flag that we wouldn't work out. I figured I could compromise on a few things, but I soon learned that she always had to get her way. Otherwise, she'd just make life unbearable until she did.

"I'll get you something to sleep in." I go to the closet to grab a t-shirt and pajama bottoms for her. "Sorry these will have to do."

"Your silk pajamas in the wash?" She quips.

"I don't wear any, but I'll make an exception for you tonight." Even in the dark, I can tell her cheeks are flush.

"Can you manage this without me?" I ask. "I think so." Her words drip with sarcasm and I love that even sick she's a little feisty. She must have needed that fighting spirit while she endured that ex of hers.

"I have to call Kate. If I don't go home, she'll assume the worst and probably call the cops."

"I'll call her for you while you change."

"Her number's in my cell the codes my birthday. I'm guessing you don't need me to tell you what that is." She sounds a little angry as she winces in pain.

"No, I don't. I'll go call her."

I leave her but I don't fully close the door, so she has some light to see what she is doing. I go to the living room to find her phone. I feel her coat pocket, there is nothing. I don't want to go through her purse, but that is where her phone is. I feel around and find it. I pull up Kate's number and hope she doesn't come rushing over here. I have to be firm about being able to handle this.

"Hey, Maddy, are you almost home?"

"Kate, it's Hawthorne."

"Is Maddy okay?" The panic in her voice makes me feel like this will get out of hand if I'm not careful.

"She got sick on the way home. We're at my place. She's staying here tonight." I use my boss voice, the one that usually intimidates people who try to challenge me.

"What? Let me talk to her. I'll be there in a few minutes to get her."

"She's in no shape to travel. She wanted me to call you to tell you she's staying here." Kate thinking this is up for discussion is ridiculous.

"I'm coming over there." Her tone mirrors mine. Man, she must be one hell of a lawyer.

"I can handle this. She said she just needs to rest." I reassure her firmly.

"Yeah at home." She's a fighter. I admire how protective she is.

"She's fine here. She can sleep in my bed it's probably more comfortable than your couch. She's changing right now. She needs clothes and whatever else for tomorrow."

"I'm leaving now." She hangs up without another word. I shake my head as I go check on Madison.

I toss her cell on the couch before going back to the room. Madison is still sitting there. She got the t-shirt on, but the bottoms were a no go.

"Do you want me to help you? I promise you I won't try anything." She looks up at me and even in the dim light I can see the hesitation on her face.

"I'm under no illusion that you'd even want to try anything Hawthorne."

She really has no clue how much I want her. I get her skirt unzipped, and I help work it off her. Not the way I pictured finally getting her out of her skirt. Then I lean down to get her legs in the bottoms. I steady her, helping her stand so we could pull them all the way up. She holds onto my arms for a moment after she gets dressed. Our eyes lock. She's different from any woman I had ever been with. I swallow hard. God, I want to kiss her.

"We need to get you into bed." I pull the blankets back so I can help her get in and situated.

"Did you call Kate?" She sounds a little drowsy.

"Uh… Yeah." I don't want her to know how upset Kate is.

"Oh no, she's on her way, isn't she?" I shake my head. "I'm sorry."

"It's fine. I think I can handle Kate." She makes a face accompanied by the sleepiest laugh.

"You do not understand what you're in for." Her eyes close as she snuggles into my bed. This is where she belongs. She is safe here and more important, this is where I want her. I smooth her hair back, tucking the covers in around her. I must be crazy, I think as I force myself to leave her to rest. Everything in me wants to crawl in bed and hold her. Not the best idea with Kate coming over. Besides, I don't know how Madison will react to me doing that. I go into the kitchen to pour myself a glass of water. I'm restless so I go into my office and get a few things done. My phone buzzes as I loosen my tie. It's the private security firm I used to help with my private matters.

"Hello."

"Hawthorne, it's Lucas. I just wanted to reach out on the info we sent you about your personal assistant. Did it help?"

"Yeah it did. Look if I needed you to find this guy do you think you could?"

"Probably. Won't be cheap though."

I chuckle. "Nothing worth it ever is Lucas."

"What are you thinking you want a face to face with him or for us to turn him over to the authorities?"

"I need him found for now. I'm not sure what to do after that. I just need a location. I want to know where this bastard is."

"We'll dig in. I will email you the contract later. Personal email good?"

"Yeah, this is an off the books thing. No one that works with me can know about this, not even my assistant."

"This guy's a real asshole. You worried about her safety?"

"Not at the moment. Once we know more, I may need other services to make sure she's safe ."

"We can help you there."

The doorbell sounds, signaling Kate's arrival.

"Look I'll be in touch just find him for me and soon."

"Sounds good!"

I end the call and go to let Kate in. She pushes past me before turning on me.

"Where is she Hawthorne?" She's all worked up.

"She's in bed resting." I hold my hands up in surrender.

"What happened?" She's trying to calm herself.

"She had a rough day. She got a migraine. It got bad on the way home. I took care of her. Now she's in bed resting."

"Why the hell did you guys come here?"

"It's a lengthy story. "

"I have time, Hawthorne." She pegs me with angry eyes.

"Come with me." I lead her to my office.

"You better not be pulling some weird power shit with her. I know she has a little crush on you even if she won't admit it. If you use your power just to sleep with her, I swear to God I'll..."

She is on my heels, but she stalls out when she sees all the files still pulled up on the monitor.

"You didn't."

"I had to look into her, I had to get a background check before I could let her in."

"She will not be okay with this."

"Oh, it pissed her off."

"She doesn't want people to know too much. It puts them in danger. She must have been sick to stay after this."

"She was. Kate, I have good intentions, I promise you. I'm not what Irina makes me out to be. I didn't sleep with my last assistant."

"I know" She exhales looking back at the monitors. "She hid so much from me. I didn't know he was doing this to her. I could have helped her get out of there before it got worse." She covers her mouth as the tears pool in her eyes. She's quiet for a moment as she tries to collect herself.

"He will pay for what he did to her. She'll never have to go through that again."

"The sad thing is I never thought he'd hurt her ever. He looked at her like she was the only girl in the room. For as long as I can remember."

I can't look at her. I don't want her to know what I'm doing. I'm afraid she'll try to talk me out of it.

"Anyway, I guess this is for you two to sort out. Just keep in mind that I'm watching Hawthorne. I won't let her get hurt again."

"I will not hurt her. I promise you."

"You better not because if you do, I will be there this time and I have excellent aim, Hawthorne."

I smile at her. She has balls threatening one of the most powerful men in the city. She did it without even blinking, which tells me she means it. It makes me respect her. It also makes me happy that Madison has such a protective friend.

"Do you want to see her?"

"Yeah, I just need to check in on her."

I lead her to my room and leave them to it. I go out into the kitchen to decide what I want for dinner. My fridge is nearly empty. I hadn't had time to order groceries. Besides, I'm used to eating out. Irina never cooked, so we ordered in a lot or went out to eat. That was when she ate. After I resolve to order takeout for tonight, I sit down to place my grocery order. I need to cook more. Once news of the break-up hit the papers, I laid low for a while to avoid all the unwanted attention. As I'm adding items to my online cart, Kate walks in. She looks serious as she squares off with me.

"Hawthorne, I want to believe you're a decent guy. I really do. Eric speaks highly of you. From what I've seen, you're respectful, but I believed those things about the last guy who promised to take care of her. Well, as you know, he nearly killed her." Her voice cracks. I can practically hear her heartbreak. "She's all I have. She is my family so if you have any ill intent or weird perverted ideas please just help me load her into a car and let's spare us both the trouble of me having to destroy your life." I stare into her icy blue eyes and I knew she already knows where she'll dispose of my body. Damn, Kate is a little crazy, but I have to admit I like her.

"I promise you I will never hurt her." I look her in the eyes. "No one else will either."

"Dean is still out there."

"I know." I'm still looking her in the eyes.

"Look, I don't want her fear and your being newly single to get mixed up into something it isn't. Someone will get hurt."

"I can keep her safe. I won't let that bastard hurt her again."

"That's not your responsibility. You barely know her."

"It doesn't matter. When I looked into her eyes that first time, I saw something. Hell, I felt something. It's been a long time since I have connected with anyone. Irina saw the connection, that's why she made a scene at the gala. Things hadn't been right between us for a while and seeing me look at someone that way pissed her off. She knew things were over between us."

Kate nodded. "Yeah well, it's not just Dean I am worried about. I didn't know Irina long but I know she doesn't take losing lying down."

"Yeah, she barged in here a few weeks ago. I haven't seen or heard from her since."

"Well, let's hope it stays that way."

The doorbell rings and I figure it has to be the food. Kate gathers her things, leaving a bag for Madison. I open the door and pay the delivery guy.

"You want to stay? I ordered a lot. I didn't know what she might want, so I went a little overboard."

"No, I should be going. I don't want Eric to know I came over here. He's been acting weird lately. I think I'll drop by his place."

I didn't know exactly what was going on with them. Maybe Eric is trying to decide which way to jump. If he isn't all in, he needs to cut ties. I'm not sure if he loves Kate, but I know I'm not getting involved. I have other things to take care of. I need to find Madison's ex and make sure he understands that their marriage is over. If he doesn't, I'll just have to figure out how to get rid of him for good.

CHAPTER SIX

Madison

I wake feeling better. It's dark in the room, but I'm alone. I can faintly hear the TV is on in the living room even though I can't tell what he is watching. I sit up. It doesn't feel like the room is spinning so I try to stand up. All good there. I carefully make my way to the door. When I enter the living room, I find him asleep on the couch he told me no one should sleep on. Cleary, he had fallen asleep while watching the baseball game. I can't help but feel bad as I look down at him. I hate that I love that with him asleep, I can admire how attractive he is. I can't see those beautiful brown eyes, but I can appreciate the rest of his dark brooding features. His hair is the darkest brown, almost black. His dark lashes are long and thick. Any girl would be jealous of them. I'd never been into facial hair, but something about his immaculately groomed five o'clock shadow vibe makes me want to feel it against my skin as he kisses every inch of me. I hate to end my open admiration of him, but I feel bad that he hasn't been able to go to bed. I lean down, brushing the side of his face softly. His eyes open slowly as his hand goes to mine. To my surprise, he brings it to his lips and kisses it. Then he pulls me into his lap. For a moment, I wonder if he thinks I am his ex in this drowsy state. I freeze, not sure what to do.

"Relax, I won't hurt you, Maddie. I just want to hold you."

I settle with my head in the crook of his neck. We sit like this for a while. Neither of us says anything. It's nice to feel safe in his arms for a while. He exhales and I sit up.

"You going to be sick?" He asks alarmed.

"No, I just figured you might be sore sitting like this." I see the urgency melt away as he smiles.

"I'm good." He sits back. "You hungry?"

"A little. I think I lost my entire lunch and part of breakfast earlier. I guess the bonus is those calories probably don't count."

He chuckles a little. "Yeah, that was a lot of vomit. I've never barfed that much, and I am considerably bigger than you, so my ratio of barf to yours should be greater."

"I aim to impress." I laugh. This time I get to my feet without him stopping me.

"I know all this talk about barf must make you want to eat more?" He chastises himself a little.

"Yes, I am running on empty." He stands, towering over me. I don't feel intimidated by his size because I don't believe he'd ever hurt me.

"Come on, I ordered food but didn't want to wake you." He takes my hand, leading me into the kitchen. There are takeout containers in the garbage. He opens the fridge and begins pulling out containers and setting them on the counter.

"You went all out. Were you expecting people or something?"

"No, I didn't know what you'd like." He runs his hand through his hair.

"So, you ordered half the menu?" I raise an eyebrow at him as I chuckle.

"To be honest, I was hungry, it snowballed." He laughs, rubbing the back of his neck.

Even his laugh is sexy to me. We both make plates and warm them before he heads back to the couch. I stop and he looks at me confused.

"I should warn you I am notorious for spilling stuff and your furniture looks too expensive to suffer me."

"I hate this couch you'd be doing me a favor." He laughs and I shake my head as I join him. "I warned you."

He hands me the remote. "You can change it."

"I'm good right where we are. Kate doesn't have sports channels, I miss this. I played every sport possible in high school." I stuff my face because I really am hungry. A few forkfuls in and I notice he is just staring at me.

"I know I am not what you're probably used to. In my defense, I tossed my cookies a few hours ago. I need these calories."

"You're like a unicorn." He smiles so big I have to look away.

"I don't even know what that means." I shake my head before I load my fork up again with some fried rice. We watch the rest of the game and after cleaning up a bit, I brush my teeth. When I walk into the bedroom, he is coming out of the closet with a pair of lounge pants over his shoulder and lord help me no shirt on. Bonus if I ever needed to, I could wash my clothes on his abs. Don't picture him all suds up, don't picture him all suds up. I kept repeating in my head as I close my eyes.

"You okay? Is it too bright in here?"

"I'm fine."

"I'll be back in a few minutes. Just need to brush my teeth." I nod and get into the bed. As I wait for him to come back, I don't know what to do with myself. I hadn't shared a bed with a man in a long time. I know I shouldn't even be thinking about it, but technically I am still married. It's not like I think he is even remotely interested in me, especially after my intimate encounter with his toilet earlier. I have to admit he is hot. What if my hormones take over while I'm sleeping? This has the potential for disaster written all over it. When he comes back, I am a bundle of nerves. I mean, I'm about to sleep next to my super hot boss who I have a slight crush on.

"Turn that lamp on for me." He hits the switch, turning the light off. He gets in next to me. Shit, this is happening.

"You okay?" He asks, a nervous look on his face. "You going to be sick again?"

"No, I don't think so."

"You know most people sleep laying down right."

I roll my eyes at him as I scoot back and try to get comfy. I lean over to shut the light off, but he stops me.

"Let's talk."

"We need the light on to talk?"

"I guess not. I just figured it'd be nice to see your face while we talk." I nod and lie down facing him. We spend a few minutes just looking at each other.

"Do you hate me?" He asks, shocking me a bit.

"No, I get why you did that. I'm not crazy about you going behind my back, but I get it." I don't meet him in the eyes because I hate talking about this.

"Would you have told me about Dean?"

"No, probably not." I admit.

"That's what I thought." He seems frustrated.

"So, where do we go from here? I mean, we're crossing into gray territory. How do we go into the office and act like none of this happened?"

"What happens between us is no one else's business. If anyone has an issue, they can come talk to me. If anyone gives you shit, you come to me. I mean it. You want to tell me what made you so upset after I asked you to lunch. Was it me?"

"No." I look away. I'm embarrassed to even tell him what they said about us.

"I'm calling bullshit. Did I come on too strong? Tell me I can take it. I'll back off." I blush as he puts his hand on mine.

"I've never been more embarrassed."

"Because I asked you to lunch?"

"No."

"Then what was it?"

"Look, it's been a long time since I felt safe with someone. I've been struggling with how I feel around you. You're easy to be around. I have a crush on you. I know I'm not your type."

"Actually, you're more my type than anyone I have ever met. There's a pull between us and I can't keep ignoring it. I don't want to."

"So, you feel this too?" He smiles. God, he is so cute I want to be normal so I can kiss him, but I have this thing with Dean looming over me. I don't want it sucking him in. He has a wonderful life, and he doesn't need me coming in and ruining things.

"We can't do anything about this. Not now. I need to end my marriage and that could take a while. I can't drag you into something that can't really go anywhere. Besides, you're my boss."

"You're not dragging me into anything I can't handle. Lots of people meet their significant others at work."

"I don't want you to feel you have to handle this. You're young, rich, and hot you will find someone who isn't a complete mess."

"God, I want to kiss you."

"You know that's not the best idea." I exhale and close my eyes.

"I know." He turns, so he's on his back. I follow suit because what I was about to admit I can't say while looking at him.

"You know what's worse, that I want to kiss you too. We should go to bed now." I turn and shut the light off.

I try to make my body forget that he is right there feeling the same way I do. Lucky for me he doesn't push our conversation further.

I fall asleep at some point. When I wake, I'm wrapped in Hawthorne's arms my head is on his chest. I look up to see he's peacefully asleep. It isn't light out yet and his alarm hasn't gone off. I don't want him to wake up holding me. As good as it feels I need to distance us a bit, especially now. I slowly pull away. Before I'm free his eyes open. He pulls me tighter against him.

"Please don't. Not yet, just give this a few more minutes than we can go back to reality, Maddie."

I say nothing I can't. The sadness in his tone breaks my heart. It feels good to be in his arms. We stay that way until his alarm goes off twenty minutes later. We get ready in separate bathrooms and meet in the living room. I put my hair up into a neat bun since I don't have the time or the products I needed to dry and style it. His eyes go to my hair, and he looks like he wants to say something but doesn't. He takes my bag and sets it down.

"I'll have Ben come back for these before he picks us up. I know you don't want anyone to get the wrong idea." He sounds a little hurt.

"Probably for the best." I prepare myself for reality.

He leads the way to the elevator. I step in and he hits the button for the garage as he stands next to me. I want so much to enjoy the heat of his body against mine for just a little longer before we forget this happened. I prepare for a reality where we have to be an appropriate distance away from each other because he's my boss. A reality where I am still technically married to Dean. Ben is waiting as expected. He seems happier than usual. It hasn't taken long for me to adore him. He is a sweet man. He reminds me of my grandfather. As we drive to the café, I can practically see the wheels turning in Hawthorne's head. I focus on my phone to avoid dealing with his preoccupied state. I read emails and make notes about what I need to do today, which seems to irritate him. I can tell that he wants to talk, but it's better if we don't. I don't want to talk in front of Ben. When we arrive at the café, he helps me out of the car as usual. Today differs slightly because his hand grazes my back as we walk in. He drops it when I stiffen. Tris is behind the counter. She smiles at us as we walk in, but I can tell she knows him well enough to know that something is off. I excuse myself to the bathroom because I need a minute alone. On my way back to the front, I see a flyer for a self-defense class on the community board. Hawthorne is on his phone when I approach the counter.

"What's happening with him?" Tris asks as she makes our drinks.

"Don't know. Hey, do you know anything about that self-defense class on the community board?"

"Yeah my brother and I run it. You interested?" She asks perking up.

"Yeah, I've been meaning to take one with my best friend Kate. Do we need to sign up?"

"No, just show up I'll make sure I save two spots."

"Cool. I'll ask if she's free, but either way I'll be there."

She brings our drinks over as Hawthorne gets off the phone. I hand him his drink and his hand lingers on mine. Our eyes lock for a moment before I look away.

"See you later, Tris." I say as I walk away. Tris stops him before he can follow. I don't wait. I text Kate to see if she can go to the class with me. It's nice out so Ben is standing by the car when I approach.

"Do you not like coffee?" I ask as I look up from my phone.

"I can't do the caffeine."

"They have other things."

"I know but I bring water with."

"Are you feeling better?"

"I think so. I get these migraines and when they get like yesterday's episode, it gets bad real fast. I'm lucky we stopped when we did, or I'd have made a mess in the back of this car."

"Do you know what causes them?"

"Severe head trauma. At least in my case."

"Accident?" He asks tilting his head.

"We ready?" Hawthorne's voice makes me jump.

Ben hadn't noticed him come outside either. Hawthorne's in a bit of a mood. We ride to the office in silence. I have so much going on and he's gone for most of the day in offsite meetings. Theo comes over and asks if I am ready for lunch. I forgot to bring something. I'm going out to get something. Theo tells me about a small deli that makes great sandwiches down the corner. We go there together. We sit out front and eat, making small talk. It's nice to get to know him a little. It's also nice to be out in the sun. It feels like such a long time since I just sat and enjoyed something so simple. He asks me basic things like if I enjoy working for Hawthorne, and if I have given thought to which of the company charity's I'll be donating my time to. I hadn't really thought about the charity thing. I enjoy working for Hawthorne. I mean, apart from his violating my privacy and those bitches in accounting, I like my job. Theo tells me he's been in the city for a few years and that he really enjoys working for Hawthorne. I get the sense there is more to their story. He isn't so stuffy once I get to know him. He tells me if I ever want a guide during lunch or on the weekend to call him. I may just take him up on that. I tell him I could use some help apartment hunting. He tells me he knows of a place that has a few openings and it is close to work. He says he'll give me the info when we get back to the office. When we return, Hawthorne's office door is closed. Something that doesn't really seem out of place. He must have gotten back from his meeting early. I go back to what I was doing before I left for lunch. Hawthorne emerges, smiling at me. Maybe he's glad this day is over.

"You ready to call it a day?"

"Yeah, let me just send this last email and I am ready to hit the road."

I finish my last sentence and hit send. Grabbing my purse, we catch each other's eye as we wait for the elevator. Burt usually leaves after us. I'm sure he is happy that we are leaving a little early. Ben's waiting as usual. I focus on anything but Hawthorne on the drive home. I just need time to process things and being around him all night and then running his life during the day has me feeling smothered. It's all Hawthorne all the time. Even with him being out of the office for most of the day, his presence looms. I just need time to detangle myself a little. I have to push down the attraction I have to him. It's a recipe for disaster. When we arrive at Kate's, Ben opens the door helping me out. I turn around to grab my bag. I find myself face to face with Hawthorne, who is stepping out of the car. "Ben, can you hang out for a minute? I want to make sure she gets up to her place okay."

He smiles and nods.

"I... I" I stutter as I look up at him.

He gives me a look. I surrender, letting him carry my bag in. We step into the elevator. I'm not sure what is going through his mind. He walks me to the door. I kept waiting for him to hand me my bag, turn around and tell me he'll see me in the morning. No such luck he follows me in. Shit! He wants to talk. We walk down the hallway and he sets my bag on the sofa. I go to the kitchen and grab two glasses from the cupboard.

"Want some water?"

"Sure."

He comes into the kitchen and leans back against the counter. I feel him watching me. When I turn, he is right there behind me, all sexy and brooding. God, I want him. I step forward and pour the water from the pitcher into our glasses, handing him one. He takes a sip before setting the glass down.

"We should talk." I take a sip of my water to deflect the nervous energy in my body.

"I don't think..." He leans forward, cupping my face. Before I can process things he's kissing me. His soft, warm lips claim mine. I liquify melting into him. I'm in another realm until I hear Kate come in calling my name. I'm so startled when I pull back I bump his glass. It shatters when it hits the floor.

"Shit!" I stumble around the kitchen trying to find the dustpan and the broom.

"Maddie, you are so accident prone." She teases as she enters the kitchen and stops short when she sees Hawthorne.

"Oh sorry. I didn't realize you had company."

"I don't. I mean. Hawthorne was just helping me with my bag."

"How nice of him." She raises her eyebrows at us. "Well, I will give you two some time to finish settling. I'll go change."

I find the broom and dustpan and begin cleaning up the mess I made. Hawthorne stops me. I can't look at him because now that

I knew what kissing him feels like, I want so much more. I want things that I have no right to want because I am still married. Until I deal with that, there is no forward for me. There is only this weird loop of uncertainty that I seem to live in at the moment.

CHAPTER SEVEN

Madison

After checking my phone for the millionth time, I decide I am pathetic. Hawthorne probably came to his senses when he left. I went to bed an hour ago and all I can do is lie here replaying that kiss in my head. I conclude that maybe I misread things. I feel like an idiot. I should be by myself for a while, not jumping into something new. I am a horrible judge of character and the fact that my heart aches over a kiss means I am not equipped to start something new. I need to stay focused on getting an apartment and completing my divorce. Ending that chapter before I start a fresh one is the best route to go. Then I can begin putting the pieces of my life back together. I check one more time to make sure I set my alarm and then I force myself to sleep. The morning drive to work will be awkward.

Ben is waiting for me like usual with a smile.

"Good morning, Maddie."

"Good morning, Ben." I climb into the car, readying myself for the holy hotness that is my boss. I'm thrown off because Hawthorne isn't there. Ben sees my reaction in the mirror.

"Hawthorne has a personal lunch meeting, so he drove himself today."

I put on my everything's okay smile and start looking through my emails hoping to hide the punch to the gut that I feel. Yep, he must have second thoughts about yesterday. I am an idiot. I think as I try to hold my tears back. When we arrive at the coffee shop, I go in feeling awkward. Tris greets me and begins making mine and

Hawthorne's orders.

"Hey everything okay?" She's studying me with a confused look on her face.

"Yeah, I'm good. How about you?"

"Okay. So, are you and your friend still planning on making it tonight?"

"Yeah, Kate agreed to try it with me. Honestly, I could use a stress reliever."

"Is Hawthorne working you too hard?" She laughs. I stiffen, wondering if she knows something.

"No." I hate feeling paranoid that he might have said something to her. "I just started apartment hunting. It's been stressful."

"Apartment hunting sucks. If I hear of anything, I'll let you know."

"Thanks. That'd be great."

"So, I'll see you tonight." She hands me both cups.

"Yep, see you later." I smile at her.

Ben opens the car door, and I set Hawthorne's drink in the cup holder. After arriving, I put my things down and take a deep breath before I knock on his office door, which is closed. The sound of a throat clearing behind me startles me and I almost drop the cup in my hand.

"Sorry Maddie, I didn't mean to startle you. Are you okay?"

"Yeah, I'm good. Nothing like a third-degree burn to wake me up."

He grabs some tissues from my desk and hands them to me.

"Is that Hawthorne's?" He gestures to the cup in my hand.

"Yeah, are you going in?"

"Yeah, he asked me to stop by. I can take that if you want to get cleaned up."

I look down and realize that I spilled a little on my dress. Thank God I'm wearing black today. After it dries, there probably won't be a visible stain. I'd just smell like coffee for the rest of the day. When I return, the door is still closed. Eric's been in there for a while, and Hawthorne doesn't come out or call me in. I figure he doesn't want to see me. I'm okay with this because it makes my day a little easier. I time my run to the copy room right around the time he's scheduled to go to lunch. When I get back to my desk, he's gone. For today this game of dodge the boss would work. It gives me some time to shake off the sting of rejection. When the day is over, Ben is waiting. I make it home with enough time to make Kate and I some dinner before we go to the self-defense class. We arrive a little early and find Tris setting up cushioned mats. She waves us in as Kate's phone rings. She tells me to go ahead. It's Eric. I walk in. That's when I notice Tris isn't alone. The guy with her is tall and muscular. Everything about him looks menacing. The tattoos running up his arms remind me of Hawthorne, and I hate the ache in my chest as I think of him.

"Hey, Maddie! You made it, where's your friend?"

"Her boyfriend called. She's out in the hallway."

"Maddie, this is my brother, Wes."

"Hi, nice to meet you." I shake his offered hand.

"Wes, Maddie is Hawthorne's new assistant."

"Yeah, he mentioned he had a new assistant last night. Nice to meet you, Maddie." His smile says it all.

Shit, he knows which means Tris will know soon enough. She'll probably hate me. It's too bad because I like her.

"Do you guys want help?"

"Sure." Tris says as she directs me on where to place mats.

"Hawthorne, send you to help since he's late?" Wes asks.

"Uh no, I didn't realize he'd be here." Shit! I try to think of a way to leave without being obvious.

"I asked him for help since our regular helper isn't available tonight."

The door to the gym opens. I turn expecting to see Kate, but Hawthorne walks in instead.

"Sorry I'm late. I had something to take care of before I got here."

He says as he finishes texting. He hasn't noticed my presence yet.

The door opens again. Kate walks in. She looks upset. I'm too pre-occupied with Kate to catch Hawthorne's reaction to me being here when he looks up.

"Everything okay?" I ask quietly.

"Eric said he needs to talk to me. It sounds serious." She looks up at Hawthorne. "Do you know what's going on with him?"

Hawthorne shakes his head. The look on his face makes me wonder if he knows something but doesn't want to get involved.

"I'm sorry Maddie, I have to go. You should stay. I can pick you up afterwards."

"I can give her a ride." Hawthorne says from behind me. The hell he will, I think.

"I'll be fine." I say as I hug her.

"Sorry Maddie, I promise we can try this again next week." I hate the nasty feeling in my stomach as I watch her leave. I go back to helping them set mats up as people arrive. I keep busy, which helps me avoid talking to Hawthorne. Every time he gets close to me, I avoid contact. Wes and Tris greet everyone before starting the class. I decide I like Tris even more while she's talking to us. She just had this way of making me feel more comfortable. We have to partner up, but my partner ditched me. I look around, not afraid to make a friend because the alternative is almost unbearable. Shit! What's behind door number three? Oh, no! Here comes my inner monologue. Hawthorne steps up. I can't look him in the eye.

"Looks like you're stuck with me." He says as I force a smile. "Thanks, my date kind of ditched me."

I stand there feeling weird. It's exactly what I've been avoiding all day. Yesterday, I reveled in the heat of his body against mine, but today after him ghosting me I want nothing more than to escape it. Tris and Wes talk through the first exercise. The first one has your attacker's hands around your throat. I can see the hesitation in his eyes as they direct us to practice. Part of me wonders if it is the awkwardness of having kissed me last night or him thinking about those evidence photos he'd seen.

"It's okay." I need to learn this. "I'm not taking this as anything other than what it is. Don't hold back on me." He takes a step forward, reaching out. His hands cup my face and our eyes lock. What the hell is he doing? I think as I move his hands down to my neck. Woo-hoo! My inner monologue shouts not having gotten the "this isn't happening" memo I'd been sending her all day. He snaps out of it as Wes comes over.

"All right, Maddie. You have six seconds before he chokes you out. What do you do?"

I follow his direction and step back, ducking out of his hold. Holy shit that was easy, I think as Wes cheers me on. "Good Maddie. Again, guys keep practicing." He says as I step around him.

"We're supposed to switch." The last place he should want my hands is around his neck because I'm still upset about last night. This might help me get over him getting me all worked up and then dumping a bucket of icy water on my warm and fuzzy's.

I step forward. My hands don't fit around his neck like his fit around mine. I do my best, but he breaks my hold. We switch off a few times, and I really feel good about my ability to get out of this hold. I loosen up as we stand there watching the next demonstration. The next one is a headlock from behind. Dean also put me in this one. Apparently, you could slip free of this one easily if you had the right moves. Hawthorne is taller than me, so we just practiced this one way. He comes at me from behind. I have to silence the part of me that likes the feeling of the heat from his body against mine. Or noticing how nice the muscles in his arms feel. That part is glad to just stay in his hold. My rational side knows I have to shut it down. As I break the hold, I remind myself that he blew me off after shattering my resolve with those soft strong lips of his. We practice this for a bit and then it is time to move to the wall. I stand against the wall with him standing in front of me. I try to focus on Wes and Tris because looking into his eyes is hard. The next choke hold has him pinning me to the wall. Yet another familiar position. This was Dean's favorite. He's bigger than me, but not as big as Hawthorne. He enjoyed trapping me. Humiliating me was something he'd gotten off on. Wes and Tris go through the moves to get out of the hold. Again, Hawthorne hesitates. He doesn't look at me as he puts me in these holds. I'm still not sure if it is because he feels weird about restraining me or if it's because of everything that's happened the past two days.

"It's okay, Hawthorne. You aren't doing anything wrong." I'm hoping he'll get over this thing.

He sets his arms on either side of my head and looks into my eyes. I'm almost sure he wants to kiss me. "Come on." I put my hands on his forearms. He nods, stepping back he puts one hand around my throat. I pivot and break his grip on me.

"Again!" Wes calls out as he walks around and corrects people. I can't help but feel like even though I am the one who survived abuse, he is the one reliving something. He doesn't make eye contact as he comes at me. Eventually, we take a brief break for water and to use the restroom. We have fifteen minutes, so I go to the bathroom and find the water fountain since I hadn't thought to bring a water bottle with me. When I go back in Hawthorne is sitting on the mat with his back to me, so I sneak up behind him. I wrap my arm around his neck, putting him in a loose hold. He reaches around and twists us. Now I'm underneath him. He looks down at me and I huff. I really thought I had him.

"I'm sorry." He says as he releases me from my pinned position.

"It's okay, nothings hurt but my ego. I thought I had you." I laugh as he helps me up.

"That's not what I mean." He says.

"Hawthorne." I sit up. "It's okay, I get it. We shouldn't have…"

"I wanted to text you last night. I got info last night on my ex. I needed to clear my head." His words come out in a rush.

"I don't know that either of us is ready for what this could be. You have some things to figure out and I just got out of something toxic myself."

"It is possible to just be friends, Hawthorne."

"I'm not so sure. I can't stop thinking about you, Maddie."

The door opens. Wes and Tris come in, stopping at the sight of Hawthorne and I sitting on the mats together. There is no doubt in my mind that we look like we are in the middle of something private because we are. We move a little further apart as they join us.

"The next half of the class might be a little uncomfortable to do with your assistant. If Maddie is cool with it, I will finish the last half with her. You and Tris can show the rest of the exercises."

"Wes, I don't think…" Hawthorne tries to argue.

"Sure!" I interrupt him before he can finish. His head flies in my direction.

"Sounds like a plan. To be honest, I think he's going easy on me." I smile at Wes. Hawthorne doesn't look amused. Wes helps me up. He leans in so no one can hear us.

"You're doing me a favor because I don't want to have to straddle my sister and vice versa."

"Yeah, that'd be a little awkward." I giggle.

"Thanks. Look, this isn't sexual at all. I don't want you thinking I'm a creep or something."

"It's all good."

"Okay, let me show you what we are doing."

We spend a minute or two going through the next exercise. I feel Hawthorne's eyes on us. I focus on the moves, trying to ignore the feeling of Hawthorne watching me. Wes is nice. He makes me feel comfortable even when he's on top of me. This didn't appear to be an attempt to get close to me or cop a feel. Just like Tris, I could see us being friends. It's weird, but I feel comfortable with them.

CHAPTER EIGHT

Hawthorne

Wes walking away with Madison is like a kick to the balls. I don't like the thought of any other man touching her. It only gets worse as the demonstration begins. Seeing him on top of her makes me jealous beyond reasoning. I have no real claim or right to these feelings. I have the overwhelming desire to tackle him and punch him in the face for touching her. I have to stop and focus on the other people we are helping in the class. I walk around coaching. The entire time monitoring them. After Irina, I have to admit I am nervous about falling for another woman who might not be loyal to me. When the class is over, Maddie and I help put everything away. Tris and Wes ask if we want to get food. I look over at Maddie and she nods. After we decide on pizza and a place, we split off. Maddie rides with me, and Tris and Wes go in Wes's car. I'm happy to have a few minutes alone with her. I open her car door and she gets in. When I settle in next to her, I can't bring myself to start the car.

"Look, I feel like we should finish our talk." I start the car.

"I think so, too." She turns toward me.

"Look, I have a lot of stuff happening right now. I'm looking for a place of my own and things are moving forward with my divorce. I am in the middle of a very complicated time in my life."

"I know and I don't want to add to that, but I can't ignore this pull between us. I don't think you can either." She shakes her head before looking up at me.

"I'm not sure if I am ready to be in a relationship right now. As much as I want the physical, I just don't know how mentally prepared I am. What if we're in the middle of something and I freak out or have a flashback? There is still so much I can't remember. It could come back anytime."

"Then we stop and figure things out. Look Maddie, I know this won't be easy. I'm a patient guy."

"Patience only go so far. To be honest, I don't know what the long-term effects of the damage he's done will be."

"What do you suggest we do?" I ask, looking over at her.

"Go with what feels right."

"What if kissing you felt right?" I ask because I'll explode if I don't kiss this woman again.

She bites her lip as her eyes move to my lips and back up. We both lean in, but I close the distance. She moans as I slide my tongue inside of her mouth to taste her. I pull back, trying to catch my breath and regain some self-control. Thankfully, the light turns green. I need to focus on driving. I take her hand as we continue our drive. I park, but I can't help myself. I pull her close and kiss her one more time. She pulls back first.

"We better go because if we don't, they'll start wondering what's taking us so long." She sits back in her seat. I turn off the car and smile as I get out. Now probably isn't the best time for us to be making out in my car.

Dinner is fun and easygoing. Wes and Tris seem to like Maddie as much as she likes them. It's refreshing being with a girl who likes my friends. Irina and my friend group weren't exactly compatible. The few times we all got together were disasters and someone always left unhappy. The other thing I love about Maddie is that we can go out and get a bite to eat without her worrying and obsessing over calories and making ridiculous requests when she orders. Even after we finish eating, we sit and talk for a while. I learn a lot about Maddie, since Tris and Wes are covering all the bases. It's like they're interviewing her to be their next best friend. Not that them liking her is bad. They tell her some of my more embarrassing moments and she is gracious enough not to tease me too much. I'm having a marvelous time. Her smile charms us all. I'm happy to get to be near her, to hear her laugh, to see her smile. It's intoxicating. At one point I just watch her in awe of how someone could go through everything she has and still be so warm. We eventually say our goodbyes and Maddie and I walk to my car. I'm not sure who made the move, but we end up holding hands. We stop in front of the passenger side door and I pull her into my arms.

"Why couldn't I have met you a few years ago?" I ask, not expecting an answer.

"I know what you mean." She looks up at me. "Two years ago, I reunited with my high school sweetheart and thought I would live happily ever after, so I was an idiot back then."

"No. I was an idiot two years ago. I started dating a supermodel who alienated me from my friends and was never happy. Then she cheated on me and thought we could work it out. How do you move past something like that? I couldn't trust her."

"Can I be honest with you?"

"Always."

"She didn't deserve you. I could tell the night I met you she was a total bitch. She dismissed me and how you treat others really says something. I knew everything I needed to know about her that night. I knew I didn't want to have any further social interaction with her."

"I'm sorry about that it was really me it had to do with. It pissed her off that I lingered when we shook hands. It's just when you and I locked eyes I felt something."

"I did too. It was like this instant animal attraction kind of thing. I know that sounds crazy."

"No, I felt it too. I thought it was just that I was over being with Irina. You two are like night and day. These past few months my attraction, it's only gotten stronger."

"We're crazy." She looks away.

"Maybe we are, but what if we aren't? What if we miss out on something amazing because of past mistakes we fear repeating? How about this we won't tell anyone at work about this? We keep it between us until we know how we feel. If it's going nowhere, we won't have to explain it once it's over."

"So, you want a 'friends with benefits' kind of deal?"

"I don't like that term."

"Why that's basically what we'd be?"

"I don't like it. I don't make out with my friends. I don't sleep with them either. You'd be my girlfriend."

"So, you and Tris have never been together?"

"No." He makes a face. "Tris is definitely off the market. Has been for years. There's no rocking that boat. Not that I have any interest there. Again, friends are off limits sex wise. If I am just friends with someone, I stay true to what that means. I don't like the gray area."

"Sorry. I didn't mean to assume."

"It's okay. Look, I'm an open book. If there's anything you want to know, just ask me okay."

She nods and I kiss her one more time before I open the door and help her in. The drive back to her place is too short for me. I don't want to say goodbye yet. I park and unbuckle my seat-belt. She stops me.

"You can't come in, Kate might be home."

"I won't. I just want to make sure you get there safely."

"What, my self-defense skills didn't impress you tonight?"

"I actually couldn't watch you and Wes go through the exercises."

"That bad, huh?"

"If I'm being honest wanting to punch my best friend in the face for touching a girl who wasn't technically mine is probably not the best look."

"It wasn't sexual. Wes is nice, but there was no tingle or vibes between us like that. Although I will say I could see us being friends. Maybe shooting hoops or going to a game or something."

"Good, because I don't share. That said, tell me more about tingles and vibes. Do I give you tingles and vibes?"

She smiles as she opens her door, leaving me sitting there. I scurry out and follow her.

"You're just going to leave me hanging?" I follow her up to the building. "At least tell me which is it?"

"Which is what?" She feigns confusion.

"Do I give you tingles or vibes?"

"Both." She shakes her head as she rolls her eyes.

I can't help but smile down at her as we wait for the elevator. We stand there looking at each other, holding hands. I like how we just fit together. Her hand fits perfectly in mine.

"See both." She bites her lip.

The door opens behind us and she pulls her hands away like mine is on fire. I look over to see Kate walking in. She's upset. She's been crying. The sting of rejection hurts. The look of concern on her face comforts my ego as she rushes over to Kate, wrapping her arms around her. They're very important to each other. I need to remember that. Kate looks up at me. I wonder is she talked to Eric. I bet she's as blindsided by his betrayal as I was. I struggled with what to do since I found out his little secret last night. One thing I'm sure of, I can't trust him and that is a problem that will bleed over into the business.

The elevator doors open. Maddie and Kate walk in. I don't follow because I know Kate needs some privacy right now. Seeing me probably isn't helping. I hope she doesn't put any of this on me, but people do weird things when they're heartbroken. Maddie looks up at me. I nod and stand there like a fool as the doors close. She'll find out exactly what went down between me and Irina, and she'd probably be feeling a certain way about me not firing Eric tomorrow. I guess I took the news better than most people would. Ever since I suspected Irina was having an affair, I began distancing myself. Deep down, I knew she was never endgame. I had just been too lazy to deal with the inevitable.

After I get back to my place, I sit around fighting the urge to text Maddie because I knew she's probably still consoling Kate. I'm about to go to bed when I get a text.

Maddie: Sorry about how the night ended.

Me: It's okay, Kate needed you.

Maddie: Yeah, Eric broke up with her. She is pretty upset about it.

Me: Did she say what happened?

Maddie: No.

Eric is the perfect example of a "wolf in sheep's clothing". He hadn't told Kate the entire truth, because if he had, Maddie would be angry. Text was the worst though because you really couldn't access emotional state from a text.

Me: That's rough.

Maddie: Yeah, I like Eric. He seems nice.

Me: Well, never judge a book by its cover.

Maddie: What's that mean? Do you know something?

Me: I know I'm not getting any more mixed up than I am now.

Maddie: I'm not even sure what the hell that means. All I know is that Kate is not okay.

Me: You can always escape to my place this weekend.

Maddie: As interesting and tempting as that is, I can't just leave her alone to deal. Eventually she'll want to talk. Besides, I got a lead on a place today. I have an appointment to look at it on Saturday.

Me: Really, where?

Maddie: A few blocks away from work. If it works out, I won't need a ride anymore.

Me: Are you trying to get rid of me?

Maddie: No. Why?

Me: It felt like you were dodging me all day today!

Maddie: I'm sorry about that. I just... I needed space.

Me: If it's too much of me. I can try to back off a little.

Maddie: No, I enjoy spending time with you. Can I be honest?

Me: I'd prefer it!

I brace myself as the bubble appears while she types.

Maddie: I thought you were avoiding me this morning when you drove yourself. I thought maybe it was a sign that you regretted kissing me. It hurt my feelings. I needed space.

Me: No, I don't regret kissing you. I'd like to do it more. I feel good when I'm around you. I had a lunch meeting. I didn't want Ben knowing who I was meeting. He doesn't exactly like Irina.

Maddie: You had lunch with her? Are you guys staying in touch?

Me: Hell, no! I just agreed to meet with her to get her to confirm some information I got. Also, so she doesn't try dropping by my place unannounced in lingerie again.

Maddie: Wow! When did she do that?

Me: Right after she heard that I hired you. I was already trying to figure out how to approach my feelings for you.

Maddie: So, you weren't even a little tempted by your supermodel ex showing up pretty much naked?

Me: No, I felt nothing. She was not happy. Now if you want to pull that same move, I think we could work something out.

Maddie: Never. Going. To. Happen! I'm not really the show up in lingerie type.

Me: Maddie, you could come over here in sweats and I would still want to fuck you.

Shit, shit, shit! I panic as I watch the bubble with the dots appear and then disappear several times. That bubble taunts me. Too much, too fast, I chastise myself. I type my apology when the bubble turn into a text.

Maddie: So, I should probably tell you now before this goes any farther...

Maddie: I have some areas of my body I don't show anyone. Areas where I can't stand being touched.

My heart sinks as my mind races to the why's of it all.

Me: I'm listening…

Maddie: My naked back is off limits. You'll never see it, even in a swimsuit. I can tolerate brief contact when I am wearing clothes, but even that's almost too much. If someone puts their hands on my shoulder from behind, it can be a trigger. If I'm being honest, I don't know what sex will be like for me.

Me: It's okay. We can take this thing slow I shouldn't have said that thing about the sex it was stupid to go there.

Maddie: It's not like I haven't thought about it.

Me: What Sex?

Maddie: Yes, sex!

Me: With me?

Maddie: Yes, with you!

Me: When was the first time you thought about it?

Maddy: The other day when you called me into your office and asked me to go to lunch. The tattoos did me in.

Me: Wait when you disappeared on me it wasn't because I was inappropriate?

Maddie: Hell no, I was so turned on I needed to take a minute to get my head together.

Me: You want to tell me what happened that day? Someone reported you crying. I honestly thought it was because of me.

Maddie: Do you promise you won't do anything crazy?

Me: I promise!

Maddie: Some women from accounting were talking about me. Saying I was a slut and basically that I was fucking you.

Me: Was one of them is a petite blonde?

Maddie: I'm not saying. I can handle it. I don't want you getting involved in this.

Me: It's my job to get involved.

Maddie: Hawthorne, I mean it! I can handle it.

Me: Fine, but if it continues, I want you to promise you'll tell me.

Maddie: I promise.

Me: Good, now get some sleep. I'll see you in the morning.

Maddie: Geez! Someone's bossy!

Me: Goodnight Madison

Maddie: Goodnight Hawthorne.

After an hour of lying in bed staring at the ceiling, I'm still awake. I can't stand the thought of Maddie being harassed at work. Especially when I have the power to stop it. Just as I suspect Irina must have reached out to Cassie about Maddie. When I hired her cousin, I had reservations. This just confirmed them. She probably asked her to spy on me. I can't fire her for that, but I can if I catch her harassing Maddie. It's one way to get rid of her. I'm all for giving people chances, but once someone shows you who they are, believe them. The last thing I need is one of Irina's puppets causing trouble at work.

CHAPTER NINE

Madison

My Friday is off to a rocky start. After Hawthorne and I text back and forth for a while, it was beyond time for bed. Kate came out of her room and wanted to talk. I stayed up and did what any best friend would do. I held her as she cried while she talked about what happened with Eric. I secretly vowed to throat punch him the next time that I saw him. It's crazy but as we talked, something came back to me something I repressed shot to the surface. Suddenly I knew exactly what she felt like. I began reliving a little of my trauma as we talked. After Dean started going off the rails, he cheated on me. The worst part is it was with his brother David's ex. She'd been hanging around Dean right after David started his second stint in jail. The crazy part is she had a son with David so why they would even go there was beyond me. It had been the final straw though. It's what finally broke me. That last thing that prompted me to leave him after all the abuse and humiliation. The betrayal had been too much. That must have been when I filed paperwork for a divorce and custody of our unborn son. Maybe that set him off the day of the attack. I still don't know why I let him in. I should have called the cops because all the paperwork I had showed that I had a restraining order against him. I guess I just figured he wouldn't hurt our child. I was wrong though. A mistake I would never forgive myself for. The attack itself was something I had yet to remember. I don't know if I want to.

I'm running late because of my lack of sleep after some past issues surfaced. Kate is taking a sick day. I don't blame her. I remind myself to check in with her this afternoon to see how she's doing.

Hawthorne looks up as I get into the car.

"Everything okay?" The concern on his face makes me feel bad.

"I'm okay. I had trouble sleeping last night."

"I'll be okay after a cup of coffee." I give him a reassuring smile.

He reaches out, taking my hand in his. I nervously look from him to our hands and then to Ben. He raises my hand to his lips, kissing it.

"Don't worry. He won't say anything. We're okay in here."

"I'm sorry." I turn toward him. "I'm trying to be open. It's hard. The truth is last night when I was talking to Kate some of my old wounds opened. Some memories came back. I guess I am reliving it. I don't even know why it bothers me after everything, but Dean cheated on me after we got married. I know we didn't get into specifics, but..."

"I am not interested in seeing anyone else." He locks eyes with me. "I'm a one-woman kind of guy. I told you I don't share. That goes both ways. When I have a girlfriend, I only have one."

"Okay. I know that women probably throw themselves at you all the time."

"Is that what's bugging you? You think I'm like Eric?" He cups my face. "Maddie, just because I have money doesn't mean I'm an asshole. In case you haven't noticed if I care about someone, I make sure they know it."

"Wait, what do you mean like Eric?"

"Nothing."

"Doesn't sound like nothing. What do you know? Was he cheating on Kate?"

"This isn't my place, Maddie. I can't."

I settle back, maybe it's better that I don't push this.

"There's so much we don't know about each other." I exhale my frustration.

He pulls me to him, kissing me softly. The noise in my brain quiets as he kisses me.

"What happened to you wasn't your fault, Maddie. I'd never treat you like he did. I don't want anyone else to treat you that way either. Look, let's get together sometime this weekend. We can spend some time together, just the two of us outside of the office. Less pressure. Tell Kate you need to help me with something."

"Oh yeah. What am I helping you with?"

"A banquet actually for the team I sponsored this summer. We wrapped up our season and Hailey quit before I could get her help to make it happen. I planned to ask you to help organize it this morning."

We pull into the parking lot and Ben opens the door for us. Hawthorne helps me out, holding my hand as we walk in. Luckily, Tris is working so when she sees us enter, she waves as she starts our order. Her eyes go to our hands and a huge smile spreads across her face. We go over to the pickup area and Hawthorne leans against the counter as we wait. He's giving me this smoldering look that makes me want to kiss him. In that moment, I remind myself someone might see us. I'm exhausted. I could fall asleep standing like this and get better rest then I got last night. I excuse myself for a quick bathroom run. I need to see if I look as crappy as I feel. Someone's in the stall, but otherwise I'm alone. I look myself over in the mirror. Yep, I look tired. I splash my face with some water. As I'm drying off, my phone rings. It's Hawthorne. I answer it on speaker.

"Everything okay in there?"

"I'll be out in a minute. I just needed to splash some water on my face, so I don't look like a woman who didn't get any sleep last night."

"Babe, you look amazing after the night you had. Tris finished our coffee so I'm ready whenever you are." My heart flutters thinking about how nice it felt to be the woman he referred to as Babe. "We have a special project to work on when we get to the office."

"I'll be right there."

I leave the bathroom feeling a little lighter. I'm excited to help plan this banquet because I know first-hand how important they are to the kids who play. I always looked forward to them. I played on every team I could. Gram and Kate made every game to cheer me on. When I get to the front, Hawthorne is talking to Tris at the counter. She smiles at me as I approach. Hawthorne pulls me against him and kisses me.

"I'm glad I have an amazing woman to help me pull it all together."

Tris leans against the counter. "Well, just between us I like her better than I liked the last girlfriend."

I feel myself stiffen, but Hawthorne's laugh turns me into putty. "So, do I." He looks down at me with those big brown eyes.

"You ready to go?"

"Yeah, I'm good." I smile up at him.

"Later Tris! Oh, tell Beck I'll be calling about wardrobe for this thing!"

"Will do! See you guys later."

"Bye." We say in unison. Look at us, not even a couple for a day, and we're already in sync.

Ben parks in front of the building. Hawthorne tells him to give us a minute. I'm collecting my things, but Hawthorne stops me.

"What are you..." His lips against mine shut down my ability to think about anything else. My entire body tingles as heat pools between my legs. When he pulls back, I'm breathless and achy.

"Hawthorne!" I try to get my brain back online.

"Sorry, I just needed one more. The thought of you being a few feet away and not being able to kiss or touch you, it's too much."

I grab the lapels of his jacket, pulling him to me. I kiss him hard and fast. When I pull away, I'm surprised to see that his eyes are closed like he's savoring the lost connection. I enjoy feeling like no matter how powerful he is, I can affect him.

"Damn babe."

"If we have to go all day. I just figured one more couldn't hurt." I sneak past him and open the door. Ben helps me out, and I thank him. Hawthorne hands me my purse and coffee, and I stand there looking at him.

"Come on, what are you waiting for? This banquet won't plan itself!"

The wicked look in his eyes confirms that he's as turned on as I am. He grabs his briefcase and holds it in front of him as we walk up to the building. He catches up to me and leans in.

"Next time you do that, don't stop."

"Oh, you can believe the next time I do that, I won't." I smile and walk into the building. I have to say I enjoy my power. Just knowing he is hard gives me a level of confidence I haven't had romantically in a while. Come to think of it, I hadn't felt like this about a man since before Dean and I got married. Even then it was never this intense. Dean and I grew up together and had common interests. Those interests made us friends, and I guess hormones did the rest. Marrying Dean seemed like the next step to things when I found out I was pregnant. It was a small wedding since neither of us had a lot of family and even Dean's twin David had missed the ceremony. Something told me Dean was having some jitters because about halfway through our reception he was more than a little tipsy. Saying I do was the biggest mistake of my life. We should have just had the baby and taken our time. In the days that followed the wedding, he became increasingly irritated by everything involving me and the baby. He started going out drinking and well, one thing led to another. Even when things had been good with Dean, it wasn't close to the attraction I have for Hawthorne.

We talk about the banquet on the way up. There are twenty kids and their family members to plan for. Hawthorne is covering all the costs and wants to make sure this is special for everyone. First, he wants me to work on finding a venue with an opening. Then we can start completing details like food, awards, and a slide show of their season. Hawthorne wants to look at multiple venues before committing. He tells me to schedule the times so we can both go. I schedule visits for Monday. Everything is falling into place. I am still waiting on a call from one venue. I pull together all the info from the season. I search for a place to create trophies and certificates. I have to admit I'm having fun working on this. Hawthorne emerges from his office as I'm going through the website I found to order the trophies from.

"Lunch?" He asks looking at me questioning.

"Sure." He smiles and my heart flutters a little. I grab my purse and my tablet because I want to go over some options for the banquet with him. The site I found has some outstanding trophies and cool looking certificates. We ride down in the elevator alone until we were halfway to the lobby. I am busy looking at the options for the trophies when the doors open. I don't look up to see who has joined us as Hawthorne takes my arm, pulling me closer to him to make room. I can feel his eyes on me, but I am focused on the screen.

"Let me see these." He leans over my shoulder to look at my screen. He smiles at me as I look up to show him the trophies. When our eyes lock, I knew he's thinking about kissing me because I'm thinking about it too. I snap myself out of the warm and fuzzy place I'm in, remembering we are not alone. I look up to see that Cassie and her friend from the other day have joined us. Cassie's friend glances at Hawthorne a few times as he focuses on the tablet in my hand. Cassie is burning a hole in my head with her mega bitch glare. I know at some point I have to deal with her. I just want to avoid taking the gloves off until I learn a little more about her. Maybe there is a history I don't know about. Hell, for all I know Hawthorne could have fucked half his staff and just be blowing smoke up my ass. The thought of him lying to me makes me a little angry. I pull away a bit at the thought of him taking advantage of me because I'm damaged goods. By the time we get to the car, I'm irrationally angry. I smile at Ben as we get in and then slide all the way over and focus on the cars passing by. Hawthorne gets in and before he slides over, I stop him.

"Don't I need space."

"Did I do something wrong?"

"No, I just need a few minutes."

"It was Cassie, wasn't it?"

"What?"

"The blonde in the elevator. Was she the one from the bathroom?"

I nod, unable to look at him. "Come here." He pulls me over to him. I can feel the tears in my eyes.

"You need to report her babe." He cups my face.

"No, I don't want someone else knowing what she said about me. I can handle this."

He kisses my forehead. "Just promise me if you need help, you'll ask for it. She's just messing with you because she's Irina's cousin." Apparently being a bitch is a family trait.

"I promise."

"All right, I'll back off about them. Don't shut me out though."

I nod. "Can I kiss you now?"

"Mmm-hmm." I smile as he pulls me in close, kissing me deep. How can a man I barely know comfort me like this? The warmth of his kiss courses through my entire body making me feel like if he never stopped, I would be okay to spend the rest of my life in his arms.

I see Ben smiling through the rear-view mirror. He is terrible. I'm sure he encouraged this from the beginning. I know I have to decide how to handle this soon because our private life would become public, eventually. Especially if we keep this up. I mean, who knows who heard his and Tris' conversation about us in the coffee shop this morning. That was stupid, especially since I don't know where this thing is going. I have to get a grip on my feelings before they get away from me and I get hurt again.

The restaurant Hawthorne takes me to is very nice. They definitely know who he is. They fall all over themselves to serve us. It's ridiculous. Hawthorne doesn't react like a man with more money than he could count. He's polite to everyone, and he appreciates the people who serve us. It makes me like him even more. Everything is going great, that is until we step out of the restaurant and run right into Irina and to my surprise, Eric. I don't know what to do or say. I slowly put together the pieces. I wasn't just angry for Kate. I'm pissed that they'd done this to Hawthorne too. I'm angry because I liked Eric. His betrayal of both Kate and Hawthorne makes me feel like I still have shitty judgment. I'm relieved that Hawthorne doesn't seem too affected. He also doesn't let go of my hand.

"Hawthorne. Maddie." Eric greets us with a smile.

"Eric, Irina." He says with a nod. He seems calm. I want to rip her hair out and punch him in the throat for what they've done.

"Hawthorne." Irina completely ignores me. Not that I care much because I am focused on suppressing the raging fire that is my anger. Hawthorne doesn't seem remotely bothered to see her clinging to Eric. Irina, however, seems nonplussed by our contact and part of me loves that it's eating her up inside. I lean into Hawthorne. He pulls me in closer. I look up at him expecting to see some hurt in his eyes but there is none.

"You ready, babe?" He asks as he smiles down at me. I nod, not wanting to speak for fear that I'd lose my resolve to stay cool. He wraps his arm around my waist, leading me out. I have to admit I like the feeling of being this close to him, but even more I love how bothered Irina looks. It serves that bitch right for not only stealing my best friend's man but for what she did to Hawthorne. We leave saying nothing else. I don't know how I will deal with Eric the next time he has a meeting with Hawthorne or God forbid I get stuck in an elevator with him at work. Ben is waiting for us. I am glad to get out of there. All of this tension is hard to process.

"You okay?" He asks, breaking me from my thoughts.

"I'm fine. I just don't understand people." I mean Eric had Kate and everything seemed fine with them. There could only be one thing that I could think of that might have gotten between them. Kate had spent a lot of her time taking care of me. I wonder if it had been the catalyst for his cheating.

"I know we don't know each other that well but I know you're upset. Was it seeing Irina?"

"No. Yes... I mean I don't particularly like her. Is Eric is the person she cheated with?"

"I didn't want to say anything but yes."

"So, you wouldn't have told me that my best friend's boyfriend was sleeping with someone else?"

"It wasn't my place. Besides, I didn't want to start our morning off with something like that. I just found out it was Eric yesterday. I had to just sit with it." He closes his eyes and squeezes the bridge of his nose like he is getting a headache.

I scoot over, touching his cheek, caressing him gently. He opens his eyes, releasing his bridge. God, he's so sexy.

"I'm sorry."

He furrows his brow in confusion.

"I know all this couldn't have been easy for you. It's not fair of me to ask so much, especially so soon. It's just with Kate, our loyalty can sometimes overshadow rational thought."

He smiles. "I like that about you two. I know she is a wonderful friend to you, especially when she threatened me the other night. I mean, I get it. I'm the same way with my friends."

"Wait, Kate threatened you?"

"Yeah, it's cool though I don't plan on pissing her off."

"I don't even know what that means."

"Come here." He pulls me closer to him. I rest my head on his chest. I love the sound of his heartbeat. Its powerful rhythm makes me feel safe, something I haven't felt in a long time. Maybe that's why I gravitated toward him that night in bed and why I am drawn to him now. He makes me feel things again. The ride back is too short for me. I don't want to let him go. We sneak in a small kiss before we go back to work. Before we need to maintain an appropriate distance between each other. I have to be careful because he doesn't have his briefcase to cover a hard on. No sooner than I sit down, my phone rings. Hawthorne smiles at me before he disappears into his office. About an hour before the end of the day, I get a call from the last venue's coordinator. I am on the phone with her when Eric comes sauntering toward me. Now's our chance! Throat punch that son of a bitch! Oh God, my inner monologue is back, and she's angry. I'm angry too. Eric has the nerve to smile at me before barging right into Hawthorne's office. I'm a little stunned to see how calm he is. My guess is he doesn't feel bad about what happened with Irina. I want to be a fly on the wall in that office because I can't imagine what their conversation must be like. After a few minutes, I half expect to hear Eric and Hawthorne fighting. It surprises me to see Eric emerge unscathed. Hawthorne appears in the doorway and my focus turns to him. I want to get up and comfort him, but that is breaking the rules I set from the moment we kissed. My body beats out my mind as I get up and go to his side.

"You okay?" I look up at him. He shakes his head and gestures to his office. My heart stops as I enter and take a seat.

"What happened?" He stands there with his back to me. I can't stop myself from going to him. I know something bad happened. When he doesn't turn and face me, I'm sure of it.

"She's pregnant. She says it might be mine."

My breath rushes out of me. I take a step back. I feel for the chair and sit down slowly. He turns, leaning back on his desk, bracing himself as his head hangs low.

"I don't think it's mine. I was very careful it's been a long time since we were together so if it's mine, it's too far along to abort."

"Wow. I um… I don't know what to say."

"I don't want to be with her Maddie. I want to see where this goes, but I need to be honest about this upfront."

"If it's yours, what do you want to do?"

"I will take care of any child I have. I want kids. This is just not how I pictured it. I want to get married and have a family, but if this baby is mine, Irina will do whatever she can to torture me."

"That means coming after anyone you're with."

The way he looks at me breaks my heart. I'm not in a place to have someone putting things out there about me. I still haven't come to terms with my past. Seeing it plastered in blogs and the papers and having people judge me for it is something I don't know if I can handle. I have to end this now. The last thing I need is Dean seeing my face being splashed across media outlets and newspapers. Even though we are over, I know it'll set him off. I'll pay the price when he gets a hold of me. He'd almost killed me once. This time he'll finish the job.

CHAPTER TEN

Hawthorne

It's funny how a day could go from good to bad in the course of a single conversation. When Eric asked if we could meet to talk, I figured he just wanted to clear the air after sleeping with my now ex-girlfriend. Life isn't that simple for me though, is it? Just when it seemed like Maddie would open herself up and let me in, the floor fell out from under us. She says that she can't get caught up in this and that once things settle in both our lives, maybe we can revisit this. Until then, I'm left to pine for her every day knowing we can't be a thing. I toss my briefcase down on the couch as I loosen my tie. I plan on hiding out this weekend. I'm not getting caught up in the shit storm until I absolutely have to. Apparently, some bloggers got wind of the pregnancy. I grab a drink and go to my office. I plan to work through the weekend. It'll take my mind off things for a while before my life became a flurry of articles and gossip news reports. No sooner than I sit down, someone is pounding on my door. I go see who it is and I'm surprised to see Kate standing there.

"What the hell, Hawthorne!" She barges into my place. She turns on me, ready to unload.

"Kate, come in." I say as I close the door behind her.

"What the fuck, Hawthorne!"

"I'm sorry. What did I do exactly?"

"You mean to tell me you haven't seen it yet?"

"Whatever you're so pissed about hasn't reached me yet. I've been a little busy having my life fall apart today."

She grabs her phone out of her purse and pulls up a photo, shoving it at me. I take it. My stomach drops. It's a photo of Maddie and I kissing. The headline read, "Billionaire playboy leaves pregnant girlfriend for the help". My stomach drops. All I can think about is Maddie and how this is exactly what she was trying to avoid.

"I need to make sure she's okay. Can you sneak me into your place? I just need to see her. Please."

She stands there for a minute like she is deciding if I deserve her help.

"It's not mine. At least I don't think it is. She was cheating on me."

"She cheated on you?"

"Yeah and I didn't want to be the one to tell you this, but it was with Eric."

"My Eric?"

I nod, feeling like shit as the shock sets in. She goes pale, stumbling back. I guide her to the couch so she can safely process the news. She puts her face in her hands and shudders as she softly exhales the pain. I feel like shit for having to do this to her, but she deserves the truth.

"It began a few months before the gala. I'm not sure how it started, all I know is it never stopped."

"You mean he's been cheating on me for months?"

I nod.

"What an asshole! Here I am taking care of my best friend who almost died, and he's out living it up with that bitch. I was such an idiot you know he used to text me to see if I was coming over. I thought he was just checking in on me, but he was probably just covering his ass."

"Look, I didn't tell you to set this thing off. I just thought you should know. I need to request a special blood test, it can help determine paternity early in the pregnancy."

"Do you really think it's Eric's?"

"Yes, I do. I haven't been with Irina in a long time and the last time

I was I wore a condom. There's a very low chance it's mine."

"If it is yours?"

"I will take care of my responsibility but I want to be with Maddie. I know that sounds crazy and I get it if you don't trust me. I just can't explain it. There's this pull between us like we're just meant to be together." She sniffles and looks up into my eyes.

"I need your word you won't hurt her. She needs protection now that this story is out if you two stay together, she'll be in the public eye. Dean might come after her. We don't know where he is, but we know what he's capable of."

"I already have that handled. I wanted to keep her out of this, but it's too late to stop this freight train once the media gets a hold of something like this. It'll snowball. I already have someone monitoring Dean's accounts. My security has his picture if he pops up in the city on any camera I will know. If he steps foot in Calgary, we'll know before he gets anywhere near her. I also have people who can provide the security she needs to stay safe. If he makes the dumbest decision of his life, we'll be ready."

"Shit, you really thought about this."

"From the moment I found out about all this I wanted nothing more than to keep her safe. That night I met her I knew, the moment I looked into her eyes I felt something. Irina saw my reaction. I thought that's what made her blow up that night, but now I wonder if it wasn't you and Eric."

"She was unusually cold to me. Do you think she's actually pregnant?"

"I don't know. We'll find out, though."

"Oh yeah, and how are we going to do that?"

"You will help me sue her requesting she provides proof she's pregnant. We ask her to submit to a DNA test with me if she is. I'm not losing Maddie, especially if this is just some pathetic attempt to trap me. I don't care what your firm charges. I need someone I can trust. My compani's legal department doesn't fit the bill."

She nods, wiping her tears. "I can do that. When we're done, we'll both have the truth. How do we know she won't pay someone to alter the test results?"

"I'll handle that. Just leave it to me. For now, I need you to get me to Maddy so I can make sure she's okay."

"How do we do that?"

"You let me drive your car back to your place and you can take mine for a joy ride. If they follow anyone, it'll be you not me. We'll meet in your parking garage. I'll head up to your place through the back."

She exhales and stands. "All right, let's go."

"Let me change first."

I go to my room and quickly make my way into my closet. I ditch my suit and grab a pair of jeans, a t-shirt and a hoodie. I wear my favorite baseball cap. Then I grab a set of car keys. When I go back into the living room, Kate looks at me a little surprised.

"What?"

"I don't think I have ever seen you dressed down. It's weird. I didn't think of you as a guy who even owned a pair of jeans."

I laugh. "There's a lot you don't know about me, Kate."

"I'm not sure that comforts me."

"Nothing bad." I hold up my hands in surrender.

"That's what they all say, Hawthorne. Do you remember what I said the other night?"

"I haven't forgotten."

"Let's go." She collects her things. Once we are in the garage, she looks at me.

"Which one's yours?"

"That row."

"You have an entire row, how silly of me. What am I driving out of here?"

"Let's find out." I click the alarm on the key fab in my hand. Her eyes widen as we walk over to the Black Audi R8 I got a few months back.

"Can you drive a stick?"

"Hell yeah." She squeals as I hand her the fab. I laugh because something tells me this is trouble.

"Don't scratch it." I smile as she gets serious.

"I swear I'll be careful."

"She hands me her keys as she gets behind the wheel. Black Subaru in visitor stall 20. Don't crash it It's almost paid off!"

"I promise I won't."

I can see the smile on her face as the engine comes to life. I run over to the lobby exit and make sure my hood is up as I exit the garage. I find the black Subaru. I get in quickly, hoping I'm not spotted. I see a few reporters have gathered, and I knew that getting in and out of the building will be a pain in the ass over the next few days. I really don't want to lead them to Maddie. I make sure I'm not followed as I drive, taking a slightly longer route to Maddie's. When I get there, I see the r8 parked in the visitor spot. I pull into the assigned parking spot for Kate. I get out and lock the car. Without looking around, I dash inside quickly and go to the stairs to avoid anyone who might recognize me. The elevator dings and I freeze.

"It's just me." I warned the front desk about potential reporters coming here. They assured me they'd try not to let anyone slip through."

She holds the door, and I follow her in. I hear sniffling as we enter her apartment. My heart breaks as we turn the corner. Maddie is standing in front of a suitcase trying hard to push everything down far enough to close it.

"Hey, what are you doing?" Kate rushes to her side. I'm frozen because I knew exactly what she's doing. She's running. She must have seen the articles.

"You can't leave me, Maddie." She looks back in shock. I hate seeing her like this. She's scared and hurt.

"You shouldn't be here, Hawthorne."

"I'm not giving up on us."

"You're crazy we barely know each other. This is exactly what I get for even thinking it would be easy to move on. I need to finish my divorce and get my life together."

"I agree but you can do that with me by your side."

"I can't. She called me you know."

"What?"

"She told me if I leave now, she'll leave me out of it but if I stay she'll make sure my past comes back for me. She will make sure he can find me. He will find me." She's sobbing. Kate makes her sit and puts her arms around her.

"I won't let that happen." I walk over, kneeling in front of her. "I promise." I take her hands and kiss them. Kate holds her at arm's length.

"Hear him out before you decide what you want to do."

She sniffles, trying to steady her breathing. I pull her to me, kissing her softly.

"Baby, listen, I will get this straightened out. I have a plan, but you need to trust me."

She nods. "I don't know where he is."

"I hired someone to find him when I found out about your past. I just wanted to know where he was and make sure you weren't in danger. I'll get an alert if he makes a move to come anywhere near here. I will be the first one to know."

"What about Irina? The baby?"

"I just hired Kate to file a request to have her prove the pregnancy and submit to a DNA test. It's not mine. I know it. We haven't slept together in a very long time. I used protection the last time we were together, so the chances are slim to none that if there is a baby it's mine."

"What if it is?"

"I will deal with that if it is mine."

"She's already dragging me through the mud. She told me she will make my past public knowledge."

"She is full of shit. She digs in and makes the abuse public, it only makes her look like a horrible person."

"She will spin this make it look like I just want your money."

"Look, we know the truth right." She nods in response. "That's all that matters." I cradle her face.

"I can't stay here. The building manager will not be happy that we have yet another security issue. I don't want Kate losing her place because of me."

"So, come stay with me."

"We barely started dating. I'm not moving in with you. I'm supposed to look at a place tomorrow."

"Stay with me until you decide. I can keep you safe. My building security gets paid very well to keep out anyone who doesn't belong there."

Kate comes back into the room. She looks from Maddie to me and back. "So, what's the plan guys?"

"I think we need to get both of you out of here." I look to Kate. "We can head to my sister's place. We'll lie low there for the night until we have a better plan."

"Sounds good to me. I could use a night away from here. I'll go pack a bag."

"Do you always use money to solve your problems?" Maddie asks, not looking at me.

"No, I don't. I grew up dirt poor. After my father died, my mother came here hoping to make a living to support us. She got a degree and worked two jobs most of my childhood. My sister and I took care of each other, mostly. We had the help of some exceptional friends."

She winces like she is chastising herself. "God, I'm an ass. I'm sorry."

I can't stop myself. I pull her to me, kissing her hard and deep. She melts. "I forgive you. Look, there's a lot we still need to get to know about each other. Let's just deal with one thing at a time. If you're feeling a certain way about things, I'd rather you say something than just go along with something you aren't comfortable with. That goes for everything if I'm overstepping a boundary you need to tell me."

"Okay. I will. Can you do me one more favor?"

"Anything Babe."

"Hold me." We sit back on the couch, her head resting on my chest as I stroke her arm. I knew she has a thing about her back. As much as I want to comfort her, I worry she'll be uncomfortable if I touch her there. When Kate is ready, I grab their bags, and we all head down the staircase closest to the parking garage door.

"Mind if we take your Subaru? I think any press out front will notice my R8 leaving and just follow us."

"No problem." Kate looks over at my car longingly.

"Another time fancy sports car."

"I promise I will let you drive that thing again sometime."

"Oh, I like him." She looks over at Maddie, who just shakes her head. I put their things in the trunk. Kate gets in the back while Maddie rides shotgun. It feels so natural to hold her hand as we drive to my sister's place. When we pull up, a slight smile spreads across Maddie's face.

"This is gorgeous."

"We grew up here. We updated it. My mom wanted to sell it, I couldn't bear the thought of losing the place I grew up. We had too many memories here. I bought it and my sister and her family live here. She's having a baby in a few months, so she needs the space way more than I do."

Before we make it up the path, Beck's opening the front door with her hand on her very round belly.

"I figured you'd show up, eventually."

"I know. I'm sorry. I've been busy."

"So I hear." She narrows her eyes at me. I let go of Maddie's hand to wrap my little sister in an enormous hug.

"I missed you Beck." I give her a squeeze. I turn to Maddie, whose eyes are on Beck's bulging belly.

"Maddie, this is my sister Rebecca."

"Beck is fine." She nudges past me. "It's so nice to meet you. I have heard a little about you." She gives Maddy a small hug.

"It's nice to meet you too." She blushes.

"Beck, this is Kate. Maddie's best friend."

"Kate steps forward and offers Beck her hand. Thanks for having us." She puts her arm around Maddie and rubs her arm. Something is throwing Maddie off. Before I think too much about what is going on with her, Wes comes to the door. He's shirtless and sweaty and slightly out of breath.

"Hey Maddie. I figured this guy would get around to bringing you by, eventually. Who's this?" He asks smiling at Kate who is just staring at him.

Maddie nudges Kate a bit. "My best friend, Kate."

"Hey, it's nice to meet you." He holds his hand out to her.

She swallows hard, and I'm sure she isn't thinking about Eric anymore. She shakes his hand and regains her composure. I smile at Beck, who is probably thinking the same thing I am. We should set these two up on a date or something. We all end up in the kitchen talking. It's nice to be back home. There's something about this place that makes me feel like me.

CHAPTER ELEVEN

Madison

All my feelings of worry and doubt fade away as I sit talking with Wes and Kate. The longer we sit there, the more I like Wes. The wheels turn in my head. I don't know him very well, but he's easy to like. I can tell Kate's attracted to him even though she swears she gave up on tattooed guys years ago. Now that she is single, the clean-cut lawyer who just broke her heart might have her rethinking things. Beck, Hawthorne, and Tris are in the kitchen talking. Now and then I find him staring out at me. It seems as if they're arguing about something. I have a terrible feeling that it might be about me. I'm sure his sister doesn't want him bringing trouble to her front door. Besides the fact that she is pregnant, this is her family home and the last thing they need are reporters showing up and camping out. I have to say it surprised me when Tris showed up. Tris and Beck are together. Hawthorne hadn't told me much about Tris, but I had to say she and Beck made sense. They seemed to orbit around each other like they could read each other's minds. Beck didn't seem happy about whatever they were talking about. Tris attempts to talk her down, but she storms off, leaving Hawthorne and Tris standing there just staring at each other. Tris pats Hawthorne's shoulder before going after Beck. He pushes off the counter and heads in my direction. I refocus on the conversation in front of me. Kate and Wes are talking about sports and she's telling him about watching me play in school. When I feel the heat of Hawthorne's body behind me and his arms wrap around me, I relax.

"Hawthorne, you didn't tell me your girl was such a badass. Kate says she was on almost every team in high school."

"She must also be modest because she didn't go into detail."

"What I told you, I played on a few teams in high school."

"Babe, you said it all nonchalant like you might have played on a team or two. Every sport is something entirely different."

"She even played on a boy's teams."

"Okay, Kate, Relax." I try to derail her from where this is heading.

"What? You kicked ass! Remember when people thought we were a thing because I used to wear your extra jersey like the guys' girlfriends did." I laugh as I nod.

"You were the most supportive girlfriend I ever had!" I wink as I giggle.

"Yeah until you guys won the championship for hockey and you and Dean went full on lip lock in the middle of the rink."

"Kate!"

"What? It was so bad I had to cover Gram's eyes!" Wes laughs.

I feel my eyes well with tears. "Excuse me." I turn, heading into the house. I run into Tris in the kitchen.

"Hey, can I use the bathroom?"

"Sure, it's down the hall first door on the left. You okay?"

I nod. "Thanks."

I make a B-Line for the bathroom and lock myself in. I stand there, bracing myself on the sink as I try to get everything I'm feeling under control. It's been so long since I thought about the pleasant times Dean and I had that I'm not sure what I'm feeling. How did my life become what it is? Why didn't things work with Dean? It was so good in the beginning. Then I got pregnant. We got married. Maybe he felt trapped by the pregnancy, by me. I splash some water on my face and take a few deep breaths. The last thing I need is to have a full-blown panic attack. I look at my reflection in the mirror. I'm not sure who is staring back at me. What have I become? The knock at the door startles me.

"Maddie, it's Kate, can I come in?"

I open the door and Kate slips in, closing it behind her.

"Babe, I'm so sorry. I didn't mean to bring him up."

"Why didn't it work, Kate? I ask myself all the time why it didn't work. What did I do? Maybe it's because my heart wasn't really in it. I go over things in my head and I just don't know why all this happened? Maybe it's not in the cards for me. I mean, first my parents died, and I made it through that. I thought I found something with Dean. Maybe a family life just isn't in the cards for me. Maybe I'm cursed to be alone?"

"Stop it. Maddie, you didn't deserve what he did to you. You deserve the best you're the most caring person I have ever met. There's a guy out there who wants to love you and if you ask me, I think you need to let him. I know what happened with Dean fucked you up, but he's not Dean. Not even close."

"What if Irina's baby is his? Who am I to take away that baby's chance at having a family? What kind of person would do that?"

"That's what you're worried about? Maddie, if there is a baby, it might not be his. I believe him about the timeline. I think Eric was sleeping with her while I was taking care of you. He'll be a great dad, but he's made it clear he doesn't want to be with Irina. You're not to blame for them not being together. She screwed that up when she cheated on Hawthorne."

"I just don't get it. Why would he want me? I am a mess. I'm still married for Christ's sake."

"Maddie, it's just a matter of getting the judge to sign off on it. When we present the evidence of all the abuse, no sane judge would hold this up. If we need to serve him and have him appear in court, we can do it and I'll be there to help you get through it."

"That's not all I'm worried about. What if he realizes he's too good for me or I'm too screwed up?"

Hawthorne is nothing like Dean. He could have anyone he wants. Why me? I need to move on with my life. I am just terrified of history repeating itself.

She makes a face as if she's thinking about how to put something. "He's rare, Maddie, but so are you. Just don't let him go before you know for sure. Come on, he's worried about you. Go out there before he comes looking for you. The three of us will not fit in this bathroom."

We both laugh at the thought of us all in the small bathroom. We go back out to the deck. He and Wes are sitting there with Tris talking. I stand beside him and he wraps his hand around my waist, pulling me into his lap. He looks at me with those big brown eyes calming me. Kate sits, and we join the conversation. Sometime later, Tris disappears to check on Beck. I have to admit it's nice just sitting and talking. It had been so long since I had been part of a group. Dean isolated me from our friends. If he didn't hang out with someone, I couldn't hang out with them. Eventually we went looking for Tris and Beck and found them getting the pull-out sofa ready. Wes rushes over, shooing Beck away. He tells her she shouldn't be doing so much. He really cares for her. Beck rolls her eyes at him and turns toward us.

"Kate, I hope this is okay for you."

"Works for me. Thank you so much for having us."

"No problem. It's nice to have people around who don't stop me from doing things every five seconds." She glares at Wes.

"Hawthorne, I have you and Madison in your old room."

Wes gives Hawthorne a look, and he chuckles. I shake my head at them because I can guess what they are laughing about.

"I better go get the bags. Wes help me out."

They disappear up the stairs, leaving us girls to talk. Tris and I already like each other, which helps.

"When are you due?" Kate asks Beck.

Beck sits in the armchair, rubbing her bump. "Two months and counting. I'm ready."

"Do you know what you're having?" I ask.

"No. We held off. We plan to do a gender reveal at the shower." She looks over at Tris.

"She's mad at me because I want to know now and she wants to wait for the reveal. We plan on doing the reveal at the baby shower, but have to wait for their mom to get back to do the baby shower. She wants to plan it even though she's not too crazy about our life-style." Tris clears her throat.

"She's getting better. She's agreed to come back earlier than expected."

"Yeah, only because Hawthorne has all this drama going on. Otherwise, she'd probably just stay out of town until right before the baby is born, just to torture me."

"Tris, can we not do this tonight? I'm exhausted." Beck says as she closes her eyes and leans her head back.

Before Tris can respond, Hawthorne and Wes come in carrying our bags. They're laughing about something and it is a welcomed interruption. Things were getting a little heavy, and I wasn't sure knowing any of this would help me. I figure I'll meet his family, eventually. Knowing about this tension only makes me more nervous for the inevitable rejection I'll face when I met his mother. It's not like I don't come with a past. Wes stops when he sees Becks face.

"What's going on down here?" He asks looking at Tris.

"Just talking about the baby shower." Tris says. She sounds more annoyed than I think she means to.

"Wes, help me up. I think I've had enough excitement for one night. I need to go lay down." Beck holds out her hands and Wes gently guides her to her feet. They lock eyes for a moment and then he looks back at Tris, who doesn't look happy. There is so much more happening here, but I don't think I want to know what that is. Hawthorne stands in the bedroom doorway. He smiles at me as he tips his head toward the bedroom. Kate gives me a look, and I shake my head at her.

"Goodnight guys." I say as I go to Hawthorne.

"Goodnight, you guys." Tris and Kate laugh.

Hawthorne closes us in, locking the door before going over to the bed. He plops down and props himself up on his elbow. I'm in awe of him. I stall, looking around. He has all kinds of trophies, certificates, and ribbons. Most of his achievements are academic and impressive. As I look around, I am reminded of just how smart he is.

"Hawthorne, this is very impressive."

"So impressive that I never had a girlfriend in high school." He cringes.

I turn toward him in disbelief. "Sure."

He drops on his back, looking up at the ceiling. He covers his face.

"Grab one of those yearbooks. You can see for yourself. I was the biggest dork."

I pull a yearbook and hold it up. "What grade was this for you?"

"Junior Year."

I flipped through and find him. He's tall and thin, but otherwise he's still a cutie. I walk over to the bed and sit facing him.

"What's so bad you were cute you just hadn't filled out yet."

"Would you have dated me?"

"If you'd have asked, I probably would have."

"Yeah right! You'd have shot me down just like every other girl did. The guys who played sports got all the girls. I was the tall, skinny, clumsy guy who had no game."

"Well, I was a lesbian so I probably wouldn't have dated you." I laugh.

"I guess we all had our baggage in high school."

I flip through the rest of his yearbook to see what clubs he was in, but he stops me.

"Don't. I don't want you to know exactly how lame I was." He reaches out and closes the yearbook. Something about how vulnerable he is being right now touches me. I put the book on the nightstand.

"You're not lame."

"Yes, I am. I never had a girlfriend in this room before. I came close in college. I planned to spend a few days with my family, but she dumped me right before vacation."

"So... I'm the first?"

"Yeah, I guess you are."

"You know what this means, right?" I smile at him.

"No. What?"

"It means that if I kiss you." I crawl over to him. "I'd be the first girl who'll have kissed you here."

"It does." His voice is strained because he's aroused. I hover above his lips as I look down at him. I hesitate because I know if I kiss him, he'll wrap his arms around me, and I don't want him to feel what Dean did to me. I'm not ready to show him that much, but I want him. I want this.

"What?"

"I want this..." I look down into his big brown eyes.

"But?"

"I'm scared to let you touch me. What if I freak out?"

"Hey. It will be okay. What if we make it so I can't touch you? You can use my belt." He looks up at me with nothing but trust. "Tie my hands together if you want to." I feel the tears beginning to form in my eyes.

"It shouldn't be this way."

"Hey, it's just until you feel safe, right? Besides, you won't hurt me."

"Please tell me you don't have some domination desire lurking around in there."

"No, I have never hit or gotten hit for sexual gratification. I'm just trying to figure out how I can make you comfortable and if me being unable to touch you makes this work, then tie me up. I trust you."

I look down at him, and I know what I want. I wanted it, the minute he looked into my eyes. Fighting this thing between us is like swimming against the current at some point, you're just too tired to keep fighting it.

"I haven't had control of anything in a long time." The realization scares me.

"Well, I rarely give up control, but I'll try if you do."

His hands go to his belt, but I stop him. I move them away and finish opening the buckle. I can do this. He watches me through low lids. His breathing is a little off. I know he's aroused by the thought of what we are about to do. With shaky hands, I get his buckle undone, and I pull the belt through the loops on his pants. He holds his hands up, pressing his wrists together. I exhale as I bind them together with his belt. I pull it to make sure it's tight enough to keep his hands in place. I kiss him as I push his hands above his head. I hold them there and return my lips to his. Kissing him is slow torture because it makes me want more from him. As our tongues meet performing this slow, sexy dance. They've become so well versed over the last twenty-four hours. I reach down and pull his shirt up, pulling back to look at him.

"Is this okay?"

"Yes." He pants, looking at my lips.

I pull it over his head. I can't take it all the way off with his hands bound, so I leave it bunched up by the belt. He lifts his head and nips at my breast through my shirt. I moan at the contact.

"You next." He says as he lets his head fall back against the pillow. I lean over, turning the bedside lamp on. Without a word, I get up and turn off the light. As I approach the bed, I shed my t-shirt on the ground. The smile that spreads across his face makes me feel like the most beautiful woman in the entire world. I climb back on the bed and straddle him, kissing my way up his stomach to his chest. I kiss a trail up his neck causing him to roll his hips against me a little. I can feel the hard length of his erection through his pants.

"Maddie, I want you so bad."

"I want you too." My lips reach his lips once more. He rolls his hips up against me and I roll mine in response. The friction between us is delicious as we begin the slow rhythmic dance with our tongues. I'm not sure how long we spend kissing and grinding, but I want more.

"Do you have a condom?" I ask as I kiss his neck.

"Wes said there are some in the nightstand." He groans as I make my way back to his lips.

"Let me check." I crawl over to the nightstand. I open it and find an unopened box. I rip it open, pull out a row and tear one off. I want to do this. I think I've wanted this from the moment he looked into my eyes. I go for the belt on his wrists.

"What are you doing?" He asks looking up at me.

"I figured it might be easier to get you undressed and put the condom on if you have the use of your hands."

"You mean you don't want to do it for me?"

"I've actually never put one on a guy before."

"We can take care of another first tonight."

"Neither of us can afford a mistake right now. I'm leaving this in your hands, literally."

He laughs, smoldering up at me. His heated gaze makes me feel a rise in my own body temperature.

"What if I want you to take matters into your hands?"

My eyes shoot up to his. "Maybe a little hands-on time would be nice."

"Untie me." I lean over him and work the belt free when he nips my nipple through the lace of my bra. I moan and brace myself against his arms as I give in to the pleasure. I pull back. "I can't get your hands free if you keep doing that."

"Sorry, I'll behave for now."

I quickly undo the belt and pull his shirt off his arms, tossing it

"Kiss me." He commands. I kiss him hard. His hands wind into my hair and then he surprises me by flipping us over so I'm underneath him. I squeal.

"This okay?" He asks looking down at me. This is very okay, I feel so safe with him.

I nod. "Before we go any further, I should warn you these walls are paper thin."

"I'll try to remember that."

"Tell me where I can and cannot touch you."

"My back and shoulders."

"Okay, so if I wanted to take these off you?" He asks, tugging at my pants as he looks down at me.

"I'd say go for it."

He looks up at the ceiling. I wonder what he's doing as his lips move. When he looks at me again he laughs. "Sorry just thanking the big guy."

"For what?"

"For you." He undoes the button on my pants. I giggle as I lift myself up a little to make getting them over my butt easier. He tosses them somewhere behind him and then stops.

"Did you want me to drape them over a chair?"

I swat him, and he feigns pain as he laughs. When our eyes lock, it's on. In a flurry of movement, he removes his pants and is back on top of me, kissing me hard and deep. I feel his erection brush against my core. I can't stop the moan that escapes me. He pulls back and rolls to the side of me. I think he senses my disappointment because he chuckles a little as he kisses my neck. I moan as his hand works its way to my breast and his lips follow. He pushes the lace back and takes my nipple in his mouth. I gasp. I haven't felt this way in so long that everything seems intense. He releases my nipple and looks up at me as he goes to the other, repeating the slow torture. His free hand slides down my stomach to the top of my panties. His hand dips beneath the fabric and his finger slides into the wet folds. I bite my lip, trying to stifle the moan threatening to escape.

I push his hand back. "I'm not sure I can keep quiet."

"Keeping you quiet could prove to be a challenge."

"I'm sorry."

"I'm not. I want everyone to know you're mine."

"I'm sure if you keep going the entire house will know what we're doing."

"I think they already know what we're doing."

He continues kissing my neck.

"I want to fuck you in my office so the entire company knows who you belong to."

I freeze for a moment. I've never been more turned on and scared at the same time. I don't want someone to claim ownership of me after what I've been through with Dean. He treated me like an object he owned and that had proved dangerous and toxic. I knew they are two people, but still it scares me.

"Hawthorne." The way I say his name causes him to pull back. He senses something is wrong. I can't look at him as he sits up.

"I'm sorry. When I'm around you, I don't always think before things come out of my mouth."

I sit up, pulling my knees to my chest. I wrap my arms around them as I rest my forehead on them. I take a few deep breaths before I look up at him.

"I'm sorry. I think I need to slow this down." I turn my face to the side and close my eyes. I'm trying not to freak out. I feel like I may throw up. How am I so torn about being with him?

"I'm an idiot."

"No, you're not." I feel the tears roll down my face. "You should find someone normal who can give you what you deserve. Someone you don't have to ask where you can and cannot touch them."

"Maddie, I want you."

I look over at him. I sniffle as he reaches over and wipes the tears from my face.

"This was going so well. I feel like I ruined it."

"You didn't."

"How about we keep some clothes on tonight? There's plenty of time to get to the naked stage of our relationship. Besides, I don't want Wes to know how sexy you sound when you come. He might try to steal you away." He leans in, kissing me softly.

"Not happening."

"Better not. My heart can't take it."

"Your heart is safe with me." I reach out and run my fingers into his hair as I look into his eyes.

He kisses me and then gets up and goes to the end of the bed.

"Where are you going?"

He goes into the closet and grabs a sweatshirt before he comes back over to the bed.

"Let's put this on you because I want to hold you tonight." He helps me into it and then pulls the covers back. We get in and he reaches over, shutting the lamp off. It's nice to just lay in his arms and kiss him. I fall asleep to the steady rhythm of his heartbeat.

CHAPTER TWELVE

Hawthorne

It's been a few weeks since Maddie moved into her place. We've been spending a lot of time together planning the banquet and we've become closer. We still haven't quite taken the plunge yet. I think she's waiting to know where things stand with Irina and for her divorce to be final. Today is the day I appear in court for the results. I drove myself to work so I can leave in the middle of the day and Burt can be there for Maddie. I hate not having my usual drive time into work with her. She seems a little distant today. I wonder if it's because she's apprehensive about the results. There is something she isn't telling me, and I hate not knowing what's bothering her. I call her into my office before I leave, but I can't figure out what's bothering her. She's preoccupied. I hate the tension. Kate is meeting me at the courthouse for the results. I'm surprised to see Wes standing there with her.

"What are you doing here? Is Beck okay?" I ask as I approach them.

"Yeah, she's fine. She's still on bed rest. She wants one of us to be here for you today and since Tris and I vetoed her coming, here I am."

"Where's your bodyguard?" I narrow my eyes at Kate.

"You're looking at him. We sent the guy assigned to me to watch after Beck. If she goes into labor someone will be there. Tris had to work."

"Good thinking."

"You ready to do this?" Kate asks.

"Yeah, let's get this over with."

All three of us head into the courthouse, and Wes sits in the waiting area as Kate and I go into the judge's chambers. When we walk in Irina and her lawyer aren't there. I assume this is a positive sign. The judge and Kate lock eyes. He directs us to take a seat.

"I received the results of the tests you requested this court order."

I would be a liar if I said I wasn't a little nervous as we sit to hear the results.

"Mr. Price as it pertains to the matter of pregnancy" he pauses. "Ms. Vonn submitted to both blood and urine tests. The findings of those tests are as follows. The urine test proved positive. The blood test proved positive the notes show that she is around eight weeks pregnant."

I exhale because if it was my baby she'd be well over eight weeks. Yes, I did the math. "It's not mine." I peek over at Kate, who looks like she is about to be sick.

"Okay, can we move forward with the DNA test? I would like to move past this and get on with my life."

"Counselor, do you have the petition for DNA testing?"

Kate stands but doesn't respond. She looks slightly out of it.

"Kate, are you okay?" The color drains from her face and she sways a little. I catch her as she faints. The judge and I get her safely to the ground and I take off my jacket off using it to prop her feet up. Kate's eyes open. She tries to sit up. I stop her and tell her to take a minute to breathe. She nods and stays put. The judge leaves to get her some water Wes peeks in and sees Kate on the floor. He heads in our direction as the judge is returning with the water. He gets stopped by a bailiff before he can enter.

"It's okay he's with us." The judge nods and the bailiff lets Wes pass. Kate waves us away as we fuss over her.

"I'm fine. It's been a busy day. I skipped lunch."

Wes helps me get her into a chair. I can't help but notice how worried he looks. It's weird considering they don't know each other that well. Other than the self-defense course and the few nights we spent out at the house, they hadn't hung out to my knowledge. It shouldn't surprise me. Wes has a history of being a worrier. Kate's embarrassed by the attention. Wes returns to the hallway once Kate seems better and we finish our meeting. She is a talented lawyer. She has all the paperwork we need to file ready. Before we leave, the judge asks Kate to stay behind for a moment to discuss another case they'd been working on. When she comes out, she has a Manila folder in her hand and a smile on her face. Wes assures me he will make sure Kate gets home okay. I am a little irritated that I have to spend more time and money proving I'm not the father of Irina's child. I need to call and schedule an appointment in the morning to give my DNA sample taken for the test. This wasn't the news I was hoping to go back to Madison with, but it is still a win. We are one step closer to being done and moving forward with our lives. When I get back, I am surprised to see Eric waiting for me in the lobby by my office. Theo is fielding calls when I get back. Madison isn't there. Eric follows me back, and I have to say I am curious to see what he has to say. We go into my office. I sit behind the desk as he takes a seat in one of the leather chairs.

"I'm here to tell you I am putting my resignation in."

"I can't say that I'm surprised."

"Well, it doesn't send a wonderful message when the boss outsources his legal needs."

"Yeah well I figured you'd be too close to this thing."

"And you think Kate isn't?"

"Kate is an excellent lawyer. This isn't just about revenge. You know she's about two months along?"

The way his head snaps up tells me he either didn't think it could be his or it wasn't in which case there was another person involved in this scenario.

"Kate's pregnant?"

"I'm talking about Irina."

He looks relieved. Maybe the thought of two women having his baby at once freaked him out. I wonder if he really thinks the baby is mine.

"If you don't mind me asking, where are you going?"

"Jacob Kensington is running for ADA and his father needs someone to replace him. I got the offer yesterday."

"Hope it comes with a pay raise because kids are expensive."

He nods and stands. "I hope one day we can move past this Hawthorne."

"I am past it. I don't hate you, but that doesn't mean we're buddies. I can't trust you."

"Well, I can't say I'm surprised. Good luck with Madison, you'll need it if her ex shows up."

"If I were you, I'd be more worried about Irina and the baby. I can handle Madison's past just fine."

He nods at me, then he turns and leaves without another word. As I stand there in the doorway, I look at Madison's empty desk and feel a pit in my stomach. I go to the front desk to ask Theo if he knows where she went. He hangs up, looking up at me.

"Hey boss. Is something wrong?"

"Do you know where Madison went?"

"She said she was meeting someone for lunch."

"Her security went with."

"Thanks. I'll try her cell."

"No problem."

I go back to my office and text her. I wait but after a few minutes I am champing at the bit to find out where she is and who she is with. I call her this time. She doesn't answer. I leave her a message telling her I need to see her later. Just in case I don't make it back in the office after my next meeting. I leave nothing about the results or Eric quitting. I have a meeting to get to, so I figure all that would just have to wait until afterwards. Before I leave, I tell Theo to let Madison know that I need her to go over all the plans for the banquet and make sure everything is ready. As I drive across town to meet Gavin, I focus on what I have to do to get this deal in motion. I can't afford to be distracted right now.

After my meeting, I still haven't heard from her. She never does this. I am terrified something bad happened. I drive over to her place. I have a key to the lobby, so I let myself in and take the stairs two at a time. It would be quicker than the elevator and besides I need to work off a little energy. I get to her door and catch my breath before I knock. The door opens, and she is in my arms before I can say anything. Her lips meet mine, and I lift her off the ground and move us inside. I shut the door behind me and turn to make sure I get the deadbolt in place. She looks up at me, taking my hand.

"Come in. Have a glass of wine with me." I let her lead me inside. She gestures to the couch, and I take a seat, watching her as she goes into the kitchen to grab another glass. When she comes back, she hands it to me and sits, tucking her feet under her.

"So, what happened to you today? I tried getting a hold of you, I left messages. You could have at least let me know you were okay. I had all these terrible things running through my mind."

"I'm sorry. I just needed a little time to clear my head."

"What could make you ghost me like that?"

"I talked to Kate." She sounds apprehensive.

"I know it's not what we expected but you know it's not mine."

"What?"

"Irina, the baby, it's not mine. She's about eight weeks, it's been longer than that since I was with her and I was careful."

"Well, at least that's over."

"No, it's not she's trying to press forward. We petitioned the court to get her to submit to a DNA test."

"Wow, looks like we both have crazy exes."

"Yeah, I'm not sure where she's going with this, but I'm trying to clear this up. I know it's putting the brakes on us."

"It's not that." She gets up and goes over to the kitchen. She grabs a manila envelope.

"It's this." She says handing it to me. "Open it."

I open the envelope and slide the paperwork out. I realize what it is as I read. "It's final." She looks like she's about to break. Something in me tells me there is a part of her and I don't really know how big a part that's sad.

"You okay?"

"Yeah, it's just weird that it's finally over. After everything I went through, it's over. It's weird somehow I feel sad about the entire thing."

"I get it. Is that why you were avoiding me?"

"I wasn't trying to avoid you. I just wanted to process the way I was feeling before I told you. I didn't know how to express all this and I wasn't sure how you'd take it. I want to be with you. I just needed to sort through the mess in my head."

"I get it. Do you want me to go?"

"No."

"Will you stay here tonight?" The look in her eyes tells me she's had a rough day. She needs me. She wants me there.

"I'd like that. You sure you want me to stay."

She smiles and sets her glass down. "I do. It's the thing I think throws me off the most I want to feel your arms around me. It makes me feel safe. Admitting that terrifies me."

I try to think of the right thing to say, but all I want to do is hold her.

"Come here." I pull her to me and she snuggles in. "I'm glad you feel safe with me."

She exhales and I feel her relax.

"I'm sorry I wasn't there for you today. I wanted to be. I just got caught up in my head."

"I get it. It's okay. So how was Kate doing when you saw her?"

"Fine, she was hanging out with Wes. Why?"

"She fainted today. She didn't tell you?"

"No, she didn't." She says sitting up.

"Relax, she's in excellent hands with Wes."

"I should call her and make sure..." She's about to get up, but I stop her pulling her to me. I kiss her and she kisses me back. It's a matter of a moment before she's pulling at my clothes. She has my shirt unbuttoned and is going for the buckle on my pants. I want her so bad. I pick her up and she squeals before I carry her over to the bed. I lay her down under me and take off her pajama bottoms. She's wearing black lacey panties. The way she bites her lip as she looks up at me makes me harder than I have ever been in my life. I stand and hook my fingers in her panties. I look to her for permission before sliding them down her legs. She nods. I take them off, tossing them behind me. Her eyes go to my erection, straining in my pants, begging to break free. She sits up and grants its wish by unzipping my pants and pushing them down my legs. Next she's tugging at my boxers. My erection springs free, jutting toward her face, begging for attention. The way she looks up at me makes my entire body tingle in anticipation. Her soft warm hand takes a hold of my hard length. She strokes me firmly before she leans forward, a smile pulling at her lips. I inhale sharply as she takes all of me into her mouth. The way she looks up at me with those big soft brown eyes only makes me want her more.

CHAPTER THIRTEEN

Madison

When I woke in the hospital after Dean attacked me, I never thought I'd be capable of trusting someone again. Hawthorne broke through all the walls I hadn't realized I had built. I want him so bad it hurts. I want to take the pressure off of him. He took the first step by kissing me, but it's me who starts undressing him. There's nothing holding me back. I'm not someone else's wife anymore. Freedom gives you a certain resolve. My past is just that, the past. I can move on from Dean. By now he is most likely someone else's nightmare. Hawthorne makes me want things I never thought I would ever want again. The way he looks at me as he slides my panties off makes me want him so bad it hurts. I'm taking what I want. If I learned one thing from almost dying it's that from now on, I would live my life to the fullest. I want to do that with Hawthorne. I've wanted him from the moment he kissed me and tonight I'm free to have him. His hesitation is frustrating. I take matters into my own hands, so to speak. I sit up and unzip his pants, pushing them down. His raging erection springs free from his boxers. I hesitate for a moment. I haven't wanted someone like this in a long time. I look up into those big brown eyes radiating their love and admiration down at me. I smile as I lean forward and wrap my lips around him. The sound he makes emboldens me. I want to show him how I feel. I begin a slow torturous stride up and down his shaft with my mouth followed by my hand. He hesitates before he gives in and winds his fingers into my hair, holding it out of the way. I lock eyes with him as I work him mercilessly with my mouth. He groans as I release him and run my tongue from the base to the tip, sucking his head in again. He releases my hair and pulls me to him, kissing me hard. I giggle as we fall back on the mattress. He smiles as he kisses his way down my body. I thank God that I took Kate's advice and got a professional bikini treatment during our spa day last week. The look in his eyes is hungry and wanting as his tongue teases my clit. I bite my lip to stifle my moan. I shudder as his tongue strokes me harder and deeper. I can't maintain eye contact as I lose myself to him. His touch is gentle. I wonder if it's because he knows what I've been through. I push the thought to the back of my mind because if I think about what Dean did I'm afraid it'll snowball into something dark and ruin this very sweet loving moment between us. I don't want to taint our first time with that part of my life. I open my eyes and look down my body at him a small part of me wonders if I am really this lucky. He adds his fingers to the mix moving them slowly inside of me. The sensation is enough to distract my brain as he works me to the edge of my resolve. My orgasm steamrolls me. I cry out his name as I struggle to catch my breath. The way he's looking down at me makes me wonder if I've done something wrong. He looks upset. I sit up and take his hand.

"What is it?"

"You're crying. Did I hurt you?"

"I didn't even realize I was. I think that was the most powerful orgasm I have ever had." I bite my lip and giggle.

"So I didn't hurt you?"

"No, you didn't." He exhales and then looks up at me with tears in his eyes. I push him to the mattress he looks confused.

"What are you doing?"

"Do you want me?" I smile down at him.

"Yes. More than anything. I want you."

"Good." I say as I straddle him.

"I didn't bring a condom."

"It's okay I got the shot."

"What? When did you do that?"

"A week after our first kiss. I just needed to protect both of us just in case we did something crazy."

"Is this something crazy? Do you think you'll regret this in the morning because if you do, we shouldn't do this? I can't stand the thought of losing you. I love you, Madison."

His declaration makes my heart soar and only solidifies what I am feeling for him.

"I love you too, Hawthorne."

He pulls my lips to his and we're a tangled mess as he flips us over and positions himself above me, hovering. He's torturing me with sweet kisses and the promise of more.

"Are you ready, Madison?" He asks as I feel his thick head at my core.

"Yes, Hawthorne. I'm ready." I look up into his eyes and I know this is right. He kisses me as he pushes forward. He's thick and long and I gasp as he slowly fills me. I've never been with anyone this big before, but this is still less painful than anything Dean did to me. He's sweet he knows this is my first time in a long time so he takes it easy. He slowly pulls back, his thrusts forward is slow and gentle. It's almost too much to take. It feels so good. I urge him on, rocking my hips against him. We pick up the pace, falling into a delicious sensual flow. What's happening between us is like nothing I have ever experienced before, and if we never stop, I would die happy in this bed with him.

"I love you." He pulls back enough to look into my eyes. The way he looks at me makes me feel human again.

"I love you too."

I pull him close, urging him to go deeper. He does and I moan. I'm so close to another orgasm.

"I'm close, babe." He groans in my ear.

"Me too. Don't stop." I moan.

He's delivering slow, deep thrusts. I slide my hands to his perfect ass and then up his back. His lips find a spot close to my ear and it's like a detonator that sets off my orgasm. I lose all control of my body as I give into the pleasure. A few more deep thrusts and Hawthorne shudders and groans. Even with my eyes closed, I can tell he's staring at me. I smile, opening them as I look up at him. He leans in and kisses me softly.

"Incredible." He turns us so we're still joined but on our sides. It was incredible, and that terrifies part of me. Maybe giving into this was a terrible idea. What if he gets bored with me and wants to move on I could lose my job and that would screw up everything I've worked so hard for?

"Stop." He cups my face, rubbing my cheek. "I can see you're analyzing this. Talk to me. Do you regret what just happened between us?"

"It's not that I regret it. It's just... if this doesn't work out..."

"You're worried that if this doesn't work out everything you've built's connected to me."

I nod, feeling guilty because I should be happy. Here I am at the start thinking about the end.

"I mean it when I say I love you, Maddie."

"I mean it too, but things can change." I can't hold the tears in anymore.

He wraps his arms around me and holds me tight.

"I don't want to be like this, but I can't help it. After everything that happened, I guess I just start looking for the worse case scenario so I can prepare. I'm sorry I don't mean to ruin this."

"You didn't ruin this. I just need you to be honest with me. No matter what."

"I will be. I promise." He kisses me on the head and buries his nose in my hair as he inhales.

"Since we're being honest, can I ask you something?" I say as he looks over at me.

"Anything."

"Will you do that again?" I bite my lip hesitantly.

"What?"

"Make love to me again."

He groans. It's the sexiest noise I have ever heard and I giggle as he pushes me back and centers himself between my legs.

"With pleasure."

We make love three more times before I fall asleep in his arms. When I wake, he's asleep beside me.

His phone vibrates on the bedside table. I reach over to see who it is. The message is from Lucas. Apparently, his private security hooked him up with a visit to see David. I look down at him sleeping and I wonder why he would want to have a meeting with my ex-husband's twin. All kinds of things race through my head. I set his phone down and lie back down, staring at the ceiling. I know he's not Dean, but how do I know he isn't capable of worse? He's rich, powerful, and smart. He has the resources to make my life hell if he wants to. I hate thinking he could hurt me, but I never thought in a million years that Dean would and he did unspeakable things to me.

"Babe, are you all right?" His voice is groggy and when I turn his eyes are barely open.

"Yeah."

"You don't feel all right." He reaches out and cups my face. That's when I realize I am frozen.

"Sorry."

"Don't be sorry, babe. Tell me what's going on."

"I was thinking. I guess I lost myself in the past."

"Did you remember something?"

"Nothing new. Just thinking about the ghosts."

He leans in and kisses me softly. "Never again, baby. I'll keep you safe. I promise."

My breath shudders as the tears slip down my face. He kisses me and I let him pull me to him. I rest my head on his chest and release all the tension in my body. For now, I am content to just live in the sunshine for a minute because I've been in the dark for too long. For all I know, he might just want to see if David has any info on where Dean is. If I'm in danger, he would be too because of how close we are. As I lie there listening to his heartbeat, I want so badly for this thing to be pure between us. I exhale and release all the tension and focus on the steady rhythm, searching for any sign that he's not what he seems. All I find as I look up into his eyes is the man who has done nothing but care for me since we met. All I can do is pray that he has no ulterior motive. I don't think I could handle losing him. I close my eyes and try to put everything out of my mind. A few minutes later, I feel myself drifting off.

The pounding knock on the door startles me. It's late and I'm not expecting anyone. I get up and turn on the light, hoping I can stop whoever it is from waking up the entire building. I open the door and Dean pushes past me.

"You're not supposed to be here." I close the door, but I don't lock it. He's not staying long. I'm done with this back and forth. We don't need him. I reach down and rub my swollen belly. Besides, I have to be up early because I finally agreed to see David. After months of him sending requests for me to visit him in prison, I finally agreed. They set the meeting for tomorrow.

"I hear you have a little meeting tomorrow. Did you think I'm was stupid? That I wouldn't find out?" He comes toward me with his fist cocked back.

I scream, jolting up in bed right as his blow would have landed. I'm sweating and trying to catch my breath. Hawthorne comes bolting out of the bathroom.

"Babe, what happened? Are you okay?" He rushes over and pulls me into his arms.

"I remembered something. I think. It could have just been an awful dream."

"What did you remember, baby?" He pulls back, looking into my eyes as he cradles my face.

"Dean showed up late, he was angry. He went to hit me. I woke up."

"You're okay, baby. I got you." He holds me close and I melt against him. I can't be sure, but I wonder if seeing his text from Lucas is the catalyst jogging a memory I suppressed to resurface.

I know one thing for sure. Hawthorne isn't the only one visiting the prison in the next few weeks. I had to keep this quiet, but I needed to know if I really had a meeting set with David or if my dream is a product of Hawthorne going to see him behind my back.

ABOUT THE AUTHOR

Angela Peña

is an American author of Puerto Rican and Italian descent. Though she is a New York native, hailing from the Bronx, she currently resides in Minnesota. She enjoys writing complex characters that struggle with the darkness inside themselves. She doesn't mind pushing the envelope and exploring the darker side of love, sex and the human psyche. After all rules are meant to be broken, lines are meant to be crossed and what doesn't kill you makes you stronger, right?

Thank You for reading!
If you enjoyed what you read please leave a review and follow me on social media. I love to interact with readers!
Where you can follow me:
WWW.FACEBOOK.COM/AUTHORAMPENA
www.instagram.com/author_angela_pena
https://www.authorangelapena.com
amazon.com/author/angelapena

BOOKS BY THIS AUTHOR

The King's Daughter: A Kings Of Havoc Mc Novel

Sloane Mitchell is the daughter of the president of the King's of Havoc M.C, John Stanton is the son of the Chief of police. There were never two people less likely to meet or fall for each other. After a freak accident, they are drawn to each other like moths to a flame. When they spend an unexpected night together their spark ignites a fiery desire neither of them can deny. Will they be burned by the flames as they break all the rules?

All Tied Up : A Kings Of Havoc Mc Novel

When Grayson Monroe transfers to the Pembroke Falls charter of The Kings of Havoc MC, he's looking forward to a change of scenery. He's grown bored with nomad life. His sister getting knocked up by his best friend Mason has left him stressed and stuck dealing with the aftermath of their bad decisions. He turns to the only thing that quiets his mind in the chaos of his life, mind-numbing sex. He goes to an underground sex club called The Garden, where he meets a dark-haired beauty with the bluest eyes he's ever seen. She's looking to even a score, and he's more than willing to be the tool she uses to do it. What they swore was just one night is proving to be harder to let go of than either of them expected. When they get pulled together by an unlikely source, they struggle to fight their attraction. He has the club to answer to, and she has a family with expectations. Will their responsibilities tear them apart or bond them together?

Printed in Great Britain
by Amazon

77912554R00079